THE FABULOUS ZED WATSON!

THE
FABULOUS
ZED WATSON!

Basil Sylvester and Kevin Sylvester

HarperCollins*Publishers*Ltd

Published by HarperCollins Publishers Ltd

First edition

HarperCollins books may be purchased for educational, business,
or sales promotional use through our Special Markets Department.

HarperCollins Publishers Ltd
Bay Adelaide Centre, East Tower
22 Adelaide Street West, 41st Floor
Toronto, Ontario, Canada
M5H 4E3

www.harpercollins.ca

Library and Archives Canada Cataloguing in Publication

Title: The fabulous Zed Watson! / Basil Sylvester and Kevin Sylvester.
Names: Sylvester, Basil, author. | Sylvester, Kevin, author, illustrator.
Identifiers: Canadiana (print) 20200359185 | Canadiana (ebook) 2020035955X |
ISBN 9781443460910 (hardcover) | ISBN 9781443460927 (ebook)
Classification: LCC PS8637.Y4175 F33 2021 | DDC jC813/.6—dc23

Printed and bound in the United States
LSC/H 9 8 7 6 5 4 3 2 1

To you, the fabulous one reading this. Remember (in the words of Oscar Wilde): "To love oneself is the beginning of a lifelong romance."
—BASIL SYLVESTER

To Basil
(And I am fully aware they are the cowriter of this book—but they still rock!)
—KEVIN SYLVESTER

*He walked by habit across the soft carpeted floor
to rattle the brass doorknob and check if it was still
locked. But as he reached that last door on the left,
he stopped. The door was open, and he was unsure
of how to proceed...*
—H.K. TAYLOR, THE MONSTER'S CASTLE

THE FABULOUS ZED WATSON!

CHAPTER 1

From A to Zed

The librarian handed me back my card. "Zed. What an interesting name."

"Thanks," I said. "I chose it myself." I lifted my hands to my chin and grinned like I was posing for a picture.

She laughed, and I knew she was cool.

You see, I wasn't born with the name Zed.

My pronouns are they/them, and that's an issue for some people.

But for Jan (that's what the librarian's name tag read), clearly not a problem.

One more reason to love your local library.

"The computers are over there," Jan said.

I bowed, gave my best cheesy smile, pocketed the card, turned around . . .

And froze.

Someone was sitting at the computer. *My* computer.

It was summer, and I'm only allowed time on the family computer for homework.

No school. No homework. No computer.

Also, no smartphone. Mom and Dad have a strict rule: "No screen until you're sixteen."

But of course, the library has computers—which is why I was there.

I looked up at the clock. Computer time was assigned in thirty-minute chunks, and the clock read 3:01.

And some kid was still sitting there, typing away.

Grrrrr.

I marched up behind the time thief and coughed. "Ahem."

No movement.

I coughed louder. "AHEM."

Nothing.

I growled and tapped the kid on the shoulder.

Finally, he turned around, and I think he was looking at me, but it was hard to tell with all the hair covering his eyes.

I pointed at the clock, tapping my foot impatiently.

His mop of hair was also hiding a set of headphones, which he pushed off his ears. I caught only a quick snippet before he muted whatever he was listening to—it sounded like a cat being tortured. Or maybe more like a looooooong, loud Bride of Frankenstein scream.

"Oh, hey, Zed," he said in a low voice.

Eek! We knew each other? My mind scanned for recognition.

Gale?

Abe?

I took a stab. "Hey, Dave."

He blinked. "Gabe."

Gabe. Right. Darn. "Sorry. Gabe."

He shrugged. "It's all good. You waiting for this?"

I nodded. Argh. My brain had blipped again. I hated that. Gabe was in my school, and he lived . . . three houses away? We'd never been friends, but I felt like I should have at least remembered his name. I couldn't even remember us having a conversation of more than five words.

"I mean, you can call me Dave if you want to."

"What?" I asked, distracted.

He swiveled in the chair and closed whatever he was working on. Judging by the screaming I'd just heard, it was probably some heavy metal chat room. He stood up, and I quickly jumped into the chair.

"Um, bye?" he said.

I gave a quick wave over my shoulder and got to work.

The keyboard wobbled a bit, and I noticed that someone had put a thick book under it to make it higher. I pulled the book out and turned to ask Gabe if it was his, but he had gone. I set it aside.

I looked at the clock. 3:03. I had twenty-seven minutes left to work on my secret project.

A website now filled the computer screen. It read, "Inside *The Monster's Castle*: A fandom site for the greatest book never published."

About a year ago, I'd come across an article called "The Internet's Weirdest Literary Conspiracy Theories." Number eleven was the story of someone named H.K. Taylor. That article led me to this site.

My fingers tingled. I logged on.

USERNAME: @TheFabulousZW
PASSWORD: VampireLove22

A twisted iron gate emerged from a thick fog. I clicked.

The gate creaked open (I quickly hit mute) and revealed a block of text, scrolling like the opening of *Star Wars*. Even though I'd read the page a thousand times, it still gave me a thrill.

The Monster's Castle.
A book written by H.K. Taylor.
A book buried by H.K. Taylor.
A book the world could not accept.

I mean, who wouldn't be hooked already?! But the rest of the story was even cooler.

It all started with a fan letter. It all ended with hurtful words and hate.

Many years ago, an unknown writer named H.K. Taylor sent a fan letter to noted playwright Tremaine Williams.

In the letter, Taylor described the idea for a revolutionary novel.

The Monster's Castle would be a Gothic romance featuring a vampire and a werewolf, alongside a host of other monsters. Its themes—alienation and fear, love and hope—would speak to those troubled times.

Williams was blown away. "I've never seen such a unique and refined voice," he declared, "and with such a deep understanding of both beauty and horror."

He immediately arranged a contract with his own publisher, Anderson & Hanson. They paid a huge advance for the time: $100,000.

The publishing world was abuzz. "Nothing is as hot as unknown potential," A&H said in announcing the deal. "Taylor's work will amaze the reader!"

But when Taylor delivered the manuscript, there was a problem.

The lovestruck vampire and the werewolf were both men. Another character, a witch, was friends with an anti-American British zombie. The book's editor demanded a rewrite. "The book, as written, will never sell," he wrote.

He returned the manuscript with a stack of letters he'd solicited from other editors and writers, who declared the book "degenerate," "sad," "scandalous" and, finally, "unreadable."

Hurt and saddened, Taylor never responded.

Instead, a few months later, a package with no return address arrived on Williams's desk.

The package contained four sample chapters, a cryptic poem, three dried blue rose petals and a note

that simply said, "Thank you for all you have done for me. Perhaps, one day, the world will be ready. Until then, I have buried all my beautiful monsters, my hopes and, as you once called it, my 'rich promise.' The root of all is hidden here. Signed, H.K. Taylor."

Taylor was never heard from again.

The world forgot about the book.

A&H went out of business.

When Williams died, years later, the package was discovered tucked in the back of a safe in his office. On the brown kraft paper package, he'd scribbled these words: "The book exists. It is out there, somewhere, if I could only crack the code to find the root."

The code remains unbroken.

The time has come.

The world is ready.

We are the Taylor legion. And our quest is to search for and find *The Monster's Castle*.

Those four surviving chapters—wow, they were awesome!

Each focused on a different monster—vampire, werewolf, witch, zombie—who all seemed real to me.

There were epic battles between monsters and humans, but who won?

There was romance, but did the monsters ever find true love?

Since the chapters were only fragments of the manuscript, I had no idea. Finding that manuscript was the only way to get answers. What I did know, however, was that the chapters had already helped me answer questions about myself.

A menu popped up and invited me to "ENTER THE LAIR."

I took a deep breath. And clicked.

CHAPTER 2

The Lair

I looked at the site member count.

It was stuck on 35.

Not much of a legion. But an incredibly friendly group. A few, like me, were nonbinary—which was nice—and all were committed.

But the site member count had been at 36 until a couple of weeks ago. That's when we'd had to kick off some jerk named @RogerStan25. I'd come across his blog—*Roger Stan: The Modern Monster Master*—in one of my many searches for monster stories with vampires or jackalopes or mermaids.

Except his monster stories were . . . awful. He actually used the line "It was a dark and stormy night" to open a short story he called "Vampira the Vampire."

"Vampira the Vampire"? I mean, c'mon!

His werewolf in "The Moon Howls at Midnight" was named Wolfy, and he seemed to spend most of his nights sitting on a rock wondering how to catch chickens.

This Roger guy did NOT get monsters at all.

And then came the ultimate crime: he posted a new story called—wait for it—"The Monster's House."

He'd lifted all of Taylor's fragments from the fan site and pretended he wrote them himself.

Plagiarism!

I exposed him to the group. But he wrote one last horrible post before we yanked him, calling us all "freaks and losers without a clue about how the real world works."

Then—presto!—he was blocked.

I felt rather proud of myself, actually. A vigilant watchdog, unmoving in the face of evil—that's me, Zed Watson. What kind of dog, you ask? Clearly, a golden retriever with a mix of poodle.

So I was now one of thirty-five, and I was happy.

For the next twenty minutes, I was lost in the site. I read and reread the chapters, the poem and the note from Williams telling the world that he believed Taylor had left a series of coded clues.

One member, @LysanderFang22 (named after the vampire in the surviving chapters), thought the clues referred to the editors and writers who had sent all those cruel letters. But they'd all been old dudes when Taylor sent them the manuscript, and all of them were now dead, including the Anderson & Hanson editor.

If they held some key to the mystery, they were no longer much use.

We all agreed that the poem itself must have some significance.

We'd considered and rejected a number of theories. Did the first letters of each stanza spell out a message? Nope. They spelled M-Y-L-I-E-T-T-H-W-H-I-F, and as much as I loved saying that out loud, it wasn't a real word.

Could it be a Caesar code, where the alphabet shifts and *A* becomes *F*, for example? Nope. That also made the poem complete gibberish.

There were some weird words in the poem, but even those didn't yield any pattern we could make out.

So what clues were hidden in Taylor's words? We were still looking.

My brain began to spin thinking about it all, so I started a deep dive into the subtopics.

There were also subheadings for each subtopic. Like . . .

Poem
   Poetic Images
     Monster References
      Ugliness—General
       Ugliness—Specific
        Other Ugliness Imagery
         Flora and Fauna

Hmmm. Someone had recently added a new sub-heading under the topic of Flora and Fauna (whatever that was).

Flora and Fauna

Places?

I clicked.

It was from @FlorAida. Ugh.

@FlorAida was always posting stuff about flowers in the fragments and the poem.

Taylor liked flowers. So what? No one had ever been able to figure out a pattern in them.

I was usually the only one who even bothered to click on @FlorAida's notes.

I looked at the clock. I had two minutes left in my block of time.

Fine.

I sighed and started reading.

"Has anyone ever considered the possibility that the weird stuff and the flowers in the poem and the fragments are actually clues about place names?" @FlorAida had written. "Some of the flowers are found only in specific places in North America. Maybe the poem and the fragments form a map, with the root/route following botanical hints?"

I looked at the info along the bottom of the screen. The note had been posted an hour or so before. No one had seen it yet, except me.

And then my brain started to explode.

Why?

Because @FlorAida had highlighted something that both Williams and Taylor had said: "The root is hidden here." But maybe they didn't mean "root" as in plants or flowers.

It was a play on words.

Root.

Route.

The route is hidden here!

@FlorAida was a genius!

I pulled out my notebook and looked at the poem.

My heart has been taken and buried away
Perhaps to beat another day.
To understand these lines it may be
That you could find it and let me be free.

Like Shakespeare's lovers of deadly fame
In the company of angels, skulls and names
Look where he fled, a blue Rosaceae sign
I lie, uncaring of passing of time.

Et in Arcadia ego, "there I also dwell"
To help my mistress with her spells
And when the day comes, it's time to sleep
I fly away with the secrets I keep.

The rallying cry of the soldier, now dead
Lying there with bullets made of lead
I walk the earth, I never rest
A secret bond hidden in my chest.

I thought that I would never care
to smell sweet moonflower in the air
yet in my soul he has lit a spark
that carries me through the dark.

Taylor wanted us to "look" along a "route."

And the clues were hidden in the poem.

The code was about specific places, and I knew right away—in my heart and in my brain—that to find the book, we needed to go see them, in person!

But what places? I needed a map.

Just as I started searching online for maps, I felt a tap on my shoulder.

I looked up.

Some old dude was pointing at the clock.

3:33.

He frowned at me.

"Jeepers!" I said. "Three minutes? Cut me a little slack. I'm on the verge of making history!"

"You're on the verge of losing your computer privileges if you don't move," he said.

I frowned and closed the site, but my mind was still racing.

I needed to get home. But as I stood up, I noticed the book that I'd moved from under the keyboard. I read the title.

Rare Flowers of the Americas.

What the heck?

CHAPTER 3

Chez Watson

I got home and hopped off my bike. The tips of my fingers were still tingling, and I was breathing hard—and not just from biking so fast.

I couldn't wait to tell everyone my discovery. I tossed my bike onto the porch and almost tore the screen door off its hinges.

"GUYS!" I yelled, but no one could hear me.

Let me explain.

I am loud.

But even my "GUYS!" was instantly swallowed up by the louder racket of dinner prep chez Watson.

My family is big. Lots of siblings, lots of noise.

And as dinner approaches, the Watson family circle grows and extends like The Blob.

It's because of my parents. They love to have people over, yes. But my mom and dad also believe that you don't turn away anyone in need. So we always have this crowd. Kids, neighbors, neighbors' dogs—you never know who, or what, will show up for dinner on a given night.

On this given night, it sounded like the circus was in town.

When I was a kid, I thought my family was just *that big*. When I turned ten, I found out that the guy I'd been calling Uncle Amir was not my uncle at all but a longtime family friend.

Dinner was a surreal experience. If you'd asked me yesterday, I probably would have said, "I wouldn't have it any other way." But today, it was hindering my mission.

In the dining room, to the right of the doorway, someone had set up a ping-pong table, and a bunch of people I didn't recognize were shrieking and swinging their paddles wildly.

On the stairs, my sister June had set up a mattress toboggan run. The lineup was long.

So was the lineup for the bathroom.

Down the entrance hallway was the kitchen. I sniffed. Delicious smells were reaching my nose, but my quest was not the food.

Cooking usually meant at least one parent was present, and that was my best bet to announce my discovery.

I marched down the hallway, dodging ping-pong balls, flying mattresses and, for some reason, my brother Zach's bunny, Mephistopheles, who was running free and skittering between everyone's legs.

"This house is awesome," I said.

My dad *was* in the kitchen, as it turned out. He was kneading his famous handmade pizza dough and chatting with "Uncle" Amir, who sat at the counter chopping mushrooms. His wife, Andie, was grating cheese, and they were all laughing about something.

Mom wasn't there. She was undoubtedly in her study working on serious lawyer things. She didn't like to be disturbed before dinner. Ha! How she avoided that in this house was a mystery to me.

"DAD, I HAVE NEWS!" I yelled, just to be heard over their loud conversation.

"Indoor voice, Zed," said my dad. "And don't interrupt."

"Oh, brother." I rolled my eyes. "In this house, that *is* my indoor voice."

He frowned at me and began chatting with Uncle Amir again.

"But I have news!" I tried again.

Amir smiled at me.

Dad didn't.

"Zed, what did I just say? Be patient. I'm talking to someone else. Wait your turn."

"But it's really important!"

"And you're being really *impatient*," he said.

"Oh, nice wordplay, Watson," said Andie.

"DAD."

He held up a finger. "Shh. Quiet, please."

"IRONY UPON IRONY!" I threw my hands up in frustration. "Where's Mom?"

"You know the rules—no disturbing her before dinner."

"I *won't* be disturbing, I'll be . . . *enlightening*."

Before he could protest, I darted out of the kitchen and up the stairs. It got quieter as I left the throng below.

My strategy had failed with Parent Number One—I had to try a different tack with Parent Number Two.

I knocked on her study door, but she didn't answer, so I just walked in. I mean, it's not like the door was locked.

She was sitting at her desk, her forehead resting in one hand, eyes squinting at the screen as she scrolled through some (probably booooring) legal document.

"Sorry, I'm busy," she said without looking up.

"MomIneedamap," I blurted.

She lifted her forehead from her palm and turned toward me.

"Zed, what on earth?!"

I probably did look a bit unhinged by this point, panting and unable to stand still. I was flapping my hands at her. She blinked like she was trying to shake the fog of many "heretofores" and "notwithstandings" from her brain.

I figured I had about twenty seconds before she stopped being confused and started being annoyed. The perfect window of opportunity.

"Mother, I need a map of the United ... States ... of ... America." I said it slowly and clearly, as if I were talking to a spooked animal. You have to appear calm in these moments. Otherwise, a parent will sense your weakness and tell you to take a few breaths or to leave and come back when you're calmer.

By then, it's too late.

I have learned this from experience.

"Your father has one in the drawer of his bedside

table, I think," she said, already turning back to her work.

Success! Parental permission to enter their room.

"Thanks!" I smiled and sped away before she realized what she had done.

She called after me, "Don't be late for dinner, though!"

No promises, I thought.

CHAPTER 4

Putting the Cartography
before the Horseradish

I stood outside their room and took a breath. I put my hand on the brass doorknob.

"Lysander rattled the doorknob to see if it was still locked," I whispered, paraphrasing a scene from chapter 1 of *The Monster's Castle*. I felt a little like my favorite vampire in that scene. He discovers a talisman that (possibly) will help him in his quest. Of course, I had no idea if it did help because . . . the book wasn't published! But I felt that it was true.

I did *not* find my talisman, the map, in my dad's drawer. There *were* some weird things in there, though, like loose coins from Mexico, Brazil, China and Vanuatu; antacid containers (empty); and an old comic with some angry duck named Howard, of all things.

"I'm a map, I'm a map. Now where would I be?" I said as I searched around the room.

I eventually found it tucked under a leg of the dresser, where Dad had put it to stop the leg wiggling.

"Eureka!" I yelled, yanking it free.

I ran to my room.

I stopped and bowed at my door. "May the ancient ones who guard the Monster's Castle speed my safe passage through its halls."

This was an incantation that a stranger had to say to enter the castle. A magic spell instead of a key! Didn't I say this was the coolest story ever told?

I walked in.

My room was a closet. Literally.

My parents turned what had been the upstairs linen closet into my bedroom. Not that I was com-plaining—it was a trade-off for not having to share with a sibling.

My tiny bed was awesome. It leaned against the wall during the day, and I pulled it down at night. It almost felt like a vampire's coffin. My Dracula com-forter was a nice touch, if I do say so myself. And I do.

My brother Jimi had designed a desk that also folded away (or would have if I ever cleaned off the top). And I think there was a rug. But between all the dirty clothes and scattered homework assignments, I hadn't seen the floor in years.

The bed sort of found its own way of settling into the pile.

So the walls were my only option for the map. I rummaged through the desk and pulled out a box of pins.

I apologized to the posters of Lysander the vampire, Yves the werewolf, Cassandra the witch and Marion the zombie. I had made them myself, based on sketches others had posted on the website. I was pretty proud of them.

But even great art must step aside for great adventure.

I smoothed out the map as best I could, then stood on my desk and used the pins to put it up. Lysander was still able to peek at me around the tip of Alaska—I could even see the rose he held next to his face.

"Perfect," I said.

The entire road map of the United States was there before me. But it had about a gazillion places on it, from historical landmarks to gas stations. Not as easy as I'd been hoping.

"Well, better get started, Zed," I said.

From under my desk, I grabbed a secret file folder that held all the stuff from the website plus my own notes. There are things I don't post on the fan site because they are just too personal, like the story I was writing about Lysander and Yves playing board games.

In a balloon.

Flying over Paris.

"Oh, Lysander," I gushed, clutching the file folder and looking at his poster, "how romantic you are."

Lysander's eyes seemed to narrow.

"Yeah, yeah," I said. "Time's a-wasting."

I pulled out my handwritten copy of Taylor's poem and read the first section out loud.

My heart has been taken and buried away
Perhaps to beat another day.
To understand these lines it may be
That you could find it and let me be free.

That was clearly Taylor talking about themselves, because it echoed the letter to Williams.

It was the next part where stuff got interesting:

Like Shakespeare's lovers of deadly fame
In the company of angels, skulls and names
Look where he fled, a blue Rosaceae sign
I lie, uncaring of passing time.

A few months ago, there had been a debate on the website about whether "I lie" meant to lie down or to not tell the truth. Several people thought it was to not tell the truth, so they spent a lot of time trying to figure out if that meant the whole poem was a misdirection.

Which is, of course, ridiculous.

Listen, if Taylor didn't want us to find the manuscript, why write the poem in the first place?

I had developed my own theory. I know monsters, and my theory was that the other stanzas in the poem were supposed to be from the point of view of the monsters, not Taylor.

Why did I think that?

The second stanza was about being "uncaring of passing time"—that is, being immortal, like a vampire.

The third was about a bat who flew away. Bats and witches.

Fourth was about a dead soldier who still walked the earth—a zombie.

Then a beast who lived in the dark and talked about a "moon" flower. That's a werewolf talking if I'd ever heard one.

But now that @FlorAida had me searching for a "route" to find the monsters, I also knew there were directional clues hidden here too.

Did the monsters name actual places in each stanza?

That was my working theory.

But I needed some help figuring out how.

One cool thing about a household our size was that there was always someone in the crowd who could answer a question.

Or as my mom put it, "Who needs Google when we've got Gaggle?"

I opened my door and saw my brother Tom clutching a mattress, ready to fly from the top of the stairs.

"Tom," I called, "if I say 'Shakespeare's lovers'?"

"Romeo and Juliet, definitely."

"And they lived . . . where?"

"Verona, obviously."

Did I mention he was an English major?

"And any idea what a blue Rosaceae means?"

"Nope." He shook his head and flew down the stairs.

Still, two out of three. Not bad.

So I had Romeo and Juliet, Verona and some weird Halloweeny stuff with skulls and angels.

"Hmmm, Rosaceae," I repeated. I had no idea if I was even pronouncing it correctly. I was saying something like rose-sick-eye. I had looked the word up online, of course, and it basically just meant "rose."

What did the blue part mean?

"Any help?" I asked Lysander, but he was silent.

I did know one other thing, though. Rosaceae wasn't *just* in the Lysander section of the poem— Taylor had also used it in "The Vampire's Grave," the Lysander chapter of the book. Lysander St. Clair, my fave, the best character in the entire history of the written word. I couldn't wait to find the missing chapters and learn more about him!

In "The Vampire's Grave," he's just been exiled from his country. He's left behind his home, a magical place known as the Monster's Castle. And he's also left behind his best friend, a werewolf.

See, Lysander's kind of a bad guy (he does bite people), but he wants to be good. The problem is that narrow-minded humans never give him a chance.

So he's on a ship to America, staring out over the bow, the full moon rising over the sea. And he hears a werewolf's howl.

Calling his name.

Is he just imagining things? Is he going mad?

It's so poetic and so tragic!

Lysander also says he misses his garden. A special garden. When he's awake, it blooms with magical plants.

This is where the Rosaceae thing gets mentioned. Except it's just some rose in his garden.

I looked up at the poster again. "Is it a hidden place name?"

No response. *Honestly*.

Sometimes I talk to Lysander when I'm working out stuff.

"Let's move on to what I do know. Romeo, Juliet and Verona. Is it possible Taylor was talking about Verona, Italy?"

I ran a hand through my scruffy hair.

"No. Doesn't seem likely. Taylor was from the

United States. All the fragments of the manuscript were set in the US. And, Lysander, you were exiled *to* the US. So I think it's a safe bet that the clues lead there."

But was there a Verona in the US?

I stood on my desk and scanned the entire map, my nose practically touching the crinkled paper.

"Bingo!" I yelled.

Actually, I yelled it twice. Because there was a Verona, Wisconsin, and a Verona, New Jersey.

They were not close to each other.

But they were the only Veronas I could find.

"So at least we've narrowed the search to a couple of states."

Lysander seemed pleased.

"Now on to the rest of the poem."

After about an hour, a pattern emerged. I love patterns. A two-second look at the awesome sweaters covering my floor is proof of that. But the pattern I discovered now was that words in each stanza linked to words in each chapter. I took each stanza and compared it to each monster's chapter. By going back and forth between the chapters and the poem, I, Zed Watson (under Lysander's watchful eye), was able to come up with a series of possible—dare I say probable?—destinations.

Verona was linked to Lysander. Which Verona? I had no idea.

The poem fragment for Cassandra the witch talked about somewhere called Arcadia.

I found Arcadia, Indiana, on the map and circled it.

But Cassandra also lived in a belfry when she was on the run from the mean humans.

So maybe Taylor wanted us to go to Belfry, Montana? I circled that on the map as well, just in case I was getting this all wrong.

Similar deductions about other monsters led me to circle a few other cities and towns.

Huzzah, Missouri.

Arcadia, California.

Cassandra, Pennsylvania.

Lysander, New York.

Marion, Ohio.

Moon, South Dakota.

A thought occurred to me as I circled: there was nothing in the clues I was finding to say where we needed to start or finish.

Was the book hidden at one of these places?

Were bits of it hidden in all these places?

I thought about the poem. Taylor had written to Williams that all the "beautiful monsters" were buried together. So that suggested there had to be one final location.

But Taylor had also left four monster-based stanzas and four linked chapters. Why?

I sat thinking for a long time.

And what I decided was that Taylor could easily have left just one clue to find the one spot where everything was buried.

Too easy.

Instead, the clues said we needed to discover a hidden route. Routes have multiple stops. Which meant, I deduced with my amazing brain, that there were four spots the searcher had to visit to find the final resting place of *The Monster's Castle*.

Or maybe eight.

I got goose bumps as I realized that Taylor had always intended to set the seeker on a quest.

When I was sure my Zed-tacular brain had figured it all out, I put pushpins in each location and tied string between them.

Then I jumped down from my desk and looked at my handiwork.

I said I liked patterns. Well, looking at the map didn't reveal anything simple, like pinstripes. It was more of a plaid. And not a particularly well-made one.

"Of course Taylor didn't make it easy," I said. "Someone would have found the book already."

But was my quest really going to involve that much traveling? Summer vacation was almost over.

"There must be a more straightforward route," I told Lysander. "Maybe I need more help from the Watson Gaggle search engine."

I was still working on a few simpler route options

when my dad yelled up the stairs, "Zed! Everyone! Dinner is on the table, and this pizza waits for no one!"

I didn't want to pull myself away from the map, but my stomach growled.

Pizza, as my dad said, waits for no one—not even an epic adventurer.

I stole one more look at the map, then grabbed a piece of paper and a marker off the top of my desk.

I wrote: "KEEP OUT! ABSOLUTELY DO NOT COME IN! IMPORTANT PROJECT IN PROGRESS. IF YOU COME IN, YOU'LL GET CURSED FOR THE REST OF YOUR LIFE!!!!!!!"

Then I stuck my sign to the outside of my door.

In case that wasn't enough to keep people from opening it, I also drew a frowning stick figure getting zapped by powerful rays from the sky. I stepped back and admired my work.

As a final touch, I drew an arrow pointing to the stick figure and wrote, "THIS COULD BE YOU! I MEAN IT!"

Then I bounded down the stairs in search of pizza . . . and answers.

CHAPTER 5

Dinner

I flew down the stairs.

I wanted to go on this road trip. Nay, I NEEDED to go, which meant that I needed permission from my parents—and one of them to drive me.

I prepared to turn my Zed charm-o-meter to 11. Then I walked into the dining room.

SLAM!

BANG!

WHOMP!

SMASH!

HEYYYYYY...

YOOOOOO...

WHOOOOOP!!!

Often, when hearing such a clash of loud noises, people are inclined to dive under their beds. Earthquakes are quieter.

But I have learned from years of experience growing up in my house that these particular noises herald the beginning of dinner. My parents were going in and out of the kitchen with waves of pizza, pasta, salads, breads, butter. They were always the last ones to sit. I'd have to be patient.

"Hey, Zed!" said a loud voice. My sister Lizzie's friend Bunny . . . I think.

I bobbed and weaved around at least ten people I'd never seen before, many of whom were scrambling to grab a chair. Most had brought something to the table, even if it was just a half-eaten bag of pretzels.

Somehow I always ended up sitting next to my brother Jimi. My dad called him the Handy One, although I thought the Messy One was more accurate. He always smelled a little bit like grease, paint or melted plastic—it depended on his latest project. Maybe that's why the chairs on either side of him were always the last ones taken.

I took a whiff of the air. Motor oil.

"Hey, Zed," Jimi said, passing me a bowl of potato salad.

Before I could scoop some onto my plate, a pair of hands shot out and grabbed the bowl away from me.

I heard my sister Mary's voice. "You gotta be fast to be fed," she said as the salad zipped away down the table. She was always coming up with dinner ditties like that. We called them Mary Mottos.

Of course, I had my own Zedi mind tricks.

"Hey, Jimi," I said, "look who just came through the door. Anais Rodriguez!"

He jerked his head around so quickly I thought he might injure himself. I reached over and switched his food-laden plate with my empty one.

It was a nasty trick. Jimi liked Anais—and had ever since they were in grade school—but there was zero chance she was ever walking through our door. She lived in a mansion in a fancy 'hood. The kind of place with seventeen bathrooms and a personal chef. In my imagination, he was French and named Antoine Fafardelle. Okay, maybe Italian.

Jimi turned back around, frowning. I think a single tear fell as he stared at his empty plate.

I almost felt bad, but my mouth was filled with a delicious vegan meatball, so I just muttered another Mary Motto: "A meatball in the mouth is worth two on the plate."

It came out more like, "MMMbtalll fmlphedg hhjgjhs ghhhela."

Finally, after about the twentieth trip from the kitchen with pizzas, salads and other treats in their arms, my parents sat down. Everyone else also seemed to have found a chair or clear spot on the floor.

"Well, good evening, everyone," Mom said, smoothing her napkin across her lap.

There was a brief but loud and joyful chorus of "Hurray for the chefs!"

I'd once tried to get the crowd to replace "hurray" with "huzzah," a cheer from *The Monster's Castle*, but I was met with blank stares. Sometimes it's hard to get people to appreciate culture.

The cheering died down.

"Thank you," said Mom. "Before we start dinner"—she shot me a look, and I immediately stopped chewing—"we must take time to give thanks."

This was my chance! Giving thanks at our house meant that each person at the table had to share a good thing that had happened that day. Mom always started.

"I settled a lawsuit today that allowed a young woman to keep her home," she said, "and also allowed me to buy some real Parmesan cheese for dinner."

This news got another cheer.

Dad was next.

"I got a lovely new book from the library today, all about the history of the union movement. It's fascinating, actually. You see, the working conditions of most inner-city—oof!"

Mom must have kicked him under the table because he stopped suddenly.

"Next," he said.

Now it was a race. With about a thousand people crammed into the house, this could take forever. The trick was to be as brief as possible so the food didn't get too cold.

"Puppy hugged me," Mary said quickly.

"Burrito for lunch," somebody said.

I quickly lost track of who was saying what.

"Still a month of vacation left before school."

"Got a date."

"Adopted kitten."

"Orchids."

Jimi was next. I didn't hear what he said because I had prepped my own speech and was ready to go.

As soon as he finished, I stood up. "Myday-wasAWESOMEbecauseICRACKEDaCODE-about*THEMONSTER'SCASTLE*andIKNOW-whereWEneedtoLOOKtofindtheCLUESsowecan-REDISCOVERthisAMAZINGBOOKandwe-needtohaveaROADTRIPcanwePLEASEgoon-aROADTRIPbecauseIhavetheMAPallreadytogo-andallweneedtodoisGETINTHECARandwewill-bebackintimeFORSCHOOL . . . So who's in for a road trip?"

There was shocked silence as I finished.

Mary rolled her eyes. "Man, that was Zeddish even for you."

Mom smiled her sweetest smile at me, though. "I love that you've broken this code, Zed. I know how much this means to you. And a road trip is an amazing idea, right, dear?" She turned to Dad.

He nodded. "Yes, Zed. But didn't you hear what Jimi just said?"

I looked at Jimi, confused.

Jimi seemed sheepish. "Um, I said that I was thankful that Mom and Dad were letting me take the car apart this month so I could get better at understanding catalytic converters and radiator construction." He shrugged.

The kid next to me resumed the thank-you chain, but I wasn't listening anymore.

Just like that, my dream was dead. When Jimi dismantled our toaster, it took him two months to figure out how to put it back together again. Even then, it toasted only one side at a time. Mom called it Jimi's Super Sandwich Solution because the outside was always toasty, but the inside was still soft enough to soak up mayo and mustard.

I called it a major screwup because who wants one-sided toast?

A car was *way* more complicated than a toaster, and I was pretty sure a car that worked on only one side was not a good idea.

We were car-less. For at least a decade, I figured. Maybe longer.

Even if, by some miracle, Jimi surprised everyone and got the whole car working again, that would still be weeks away.

There was no way Mom and Dad would let me go on a trip once school started up again.

I slumped into my chair.

"Sorry, Zed," Jimi said. "About the car too."

Too? I looked at my plate. Empty. Jimi had done a reverse switcheroo and grabbed his plate back while I was standing up.

My lips trembled as I slid my chair back and walked slowly out to the garden.

CHAPTER 6

In the Garden

The sun was setting behind the distant skyscrapers.

Usually I can stare at a beautiful sunset for hours. Watch the clouds turn from pink to orange to purple to gray.

But today, I just didn't care.

I sat down on the porch stairs. There was a shuffling in the garden. Maybe a rabid raccoon was about to attack me. That would be fitting. Why not end the day by catching rabies?

"Hey, Zed."

A talking raccoon?

The mop-headed kid from the library emerged from behind a big bush with blue flowers. The knees on his pants were muddy. So were his hands.

Gabe? Here?

"Gabe? Here?" I said.

"Um, I was sitting across from you at dinner."

Oh. I hadn't noticed that. "Why are you out here?" I asked. "All the bathrooms full, so you decided to pee in the bushes?"

Gabe looked around at the garden. "No."

Now I remembered why our conversations had always been so short and unmemorable—they were short and unmemorable. Gabe also didn't smile much. If conversation were a competition, he wasn't even playing. But never let it be said that Zed Watson can't, as my mom puts it, "cajole a conversation from a rock."

Gabe was as rock-like as any person I knew.

I rolled my hand in the universal sign for "Please explain, and give more than one-word answers"— and I also said this out loud, which helped.

"Oh, yeah. Your mom and dad hired me to do some garden stuff. After your sister grabbed the last dumpling from my plate, I figured I'd come outside. It's nice out here. That *Hydrangea macrophylla* is really quite lovely." He motioned toward the big blue thing.

"That's what it's called?"

He nodded. "The scientific name anyway. It's just called a blue hydrangea in English."

"I'll take your weird for it."

He smiled for maybe the first time ever.

"What are you smiling at?"

"You said you'd take my 'weird' for it. I kind of like that. It's funny."

"I did?"

He nodded again. The smile vanished. He walked over and started sniffing a rose. Or I think it was a rose.

"So why are *you* out here, Zed? Bathrooms all full?"

A joke? From Gabe? What was happening?

"No, haha. I just—" I stopped for a long sigh. "I figured out something today and I was just really excited, and then my stupid brother messed everything up." I gave a quick explanation of Jimi's tragic dream of becoming a mechanic. "And now I'll never find this super-important book no one has ever heard of—"

"*The Monster's Castle*," Gabe said.

My jaw dropped. "How the heck do YOU know about that?"

"I love that book. Well, the parts we have, anyway. It's got all this amazing stuff in there about flowers and botany and science."

"It's about monsters," I said. "Monsters."

"Yeah, I'm not so much into that stuff. I mean, it's cool, but I like all the science in there."

"But how did you even hear about it?"

"I was over for dinner about a year ago, and I think you had just found out about it and were telling everyone how cool the book was. So I checked out the fan site you mentioned—"

The truth hit me like a ton of bricks.

"You're @FlorAida!" I said.

He looked sheepish. "It sounds weird when you say it like that."

"Like what? It looks like someone tried to spell Florida but stumbled on the keyboard. What the heck does it even mean? It's not anything from the book."

"Well, it's a mix of things I like. You know, flora . . . flowers. That's all in the book."

"And is Ida your mom?"

Gabe turned back to the flowers. "No."

"A heavy metal band?"

He shook his head. "Um, no. Why would you think—"

"Never mind. So *you* were the one who posted the bit about the poem maybe being a map?!"

"Yeah. At first, I thought the 'root' thing was about flowers. But there's no pattern I could see in the text. So I think it's a—"

"Play on words." We said this together.

"Yeah. The flowers are clues."

"No," I corrected him, "the *monsters* are the key to figuring out the clues."

"No, I'm pretty sure it's plants. Like, there's this bit in the fragment of the weredog chapter that mentions this really rare flower that's found only in the southwestern US."

"It's wereWOLF, not weredog."

"Sorry."

Gabe stared at his feet, and I stared at him. There was no way he could love this book as much as I did. Could he?

46

He *had* seen something in the text that I hadn't seen, though.

But Gabe was clearly hopeless when it came to understanding monsters. I clearly wasn't.

The sunset was now blazing orange. My mind began to blaze orange in full Zed mode.

"Gabe," I said finally, "I have an idea."

"Cool." He was still staring at his shoes.

I could tell one thing for sure: Gabe wasn't the go-go-go type.

He needed a dose of Zed-thusiasm.

"Darn right it's cool! Maybe the plants tell you *generally* where stuff is. But by working with the monsters, I've found, like, *specific* place names."

He looked up!

"And?"

"What if we combined them? What if knowing both those things will help us narrow it down? How are you with maps?"

I quickly filled him in on the mapping I'd done before dinner.

"The flower stuff might help," I said. "I'm a monster expert, but maybe that's not enough—incredible as that seems. Maybe if we work together, we can figure out the right route?"

"Wait, so you're saying that you have a bunch of place names but don't know which one is right? And you want me to look at them and see if the plants I'm talking about grow in those places so we can figure it out?" Gabe was smiling now. He was practically on fire!

"You got it, Flor-eye-whatever. Let's go finish this map together!"

"Sure."

I stood up, beaming.

Then my spirits fell, fast.

"ARRRRRRR! I forgot about Jimi and the stupid car."

That's when Gabe said some powerful magic words.

"My sister, Sam, has a car."

My head shot up.

"And?"

"And she's heading back to school in a few days."

My fingers tingled. "Okay . . . where, exactly?"

"Arizona State University. She's driving in what I think might be the right direction, at least based on the plant clues."

"Maybe we can go with her?"

Gabe looked down at his shoes. "Zed, what's more important—that the book is found, or that you find it first?"

What kind of question was that?

"I want the book found. I want the world to read it. *I* want to read it. I want to hold it in my hands." But now that I'd answered the first part of Gabe's question, I had to admit . . . "And yes, part of me does want to be the first person to find it."

"Me too. I'll ask Sam."

I stood up quickly and hugged him. "Gabe! This might just be the start of a beautiful friendship."

CHAPTER 7

A Beautiful Friendship

We made our way back through the sea of humanity, pizza crusts, pasta plates and dinner rolls up to the second floor.

My older brother Frank was gazing at the sign on my door.

He was laughing.

"What's so funny?" I asked.

Frank turned. He had a huge grin slapped on his face.

"Oh, hey, Gabe," he said.

"Hey."

"Frank, I asked you a question," I said.

My brother rolled his eyes. "Zed, you can be so weird sometimes."

"I'll take that as a compliment."

"You might as well. It reminds me of the night you came out as nonbinary." He started laughing so hard he couldn't talk.

I gritted my teeth. I knew what was coming. This had become Watson family lore. My coming out wasn't what he found funny. In fact, Frank often said it was only the third most interesting thing I'd done that night. (My family had been amazing.) But what had become legend was . . .

"Zed was wearing this incredibly ugly sweater. Gabe, it was hilarious."

"It was supposed to be a rainbow flag," I said, eyes narrowed.

"Except you washed it in hot water the night before and all the colors ran! You looked like a demented unicorn turd! Hahahahahaha!"

Gabe, I suddenly noticed, was frowning slightly.

"Yeah. I've done that too," he said. "Easy mistake."

Frank, seeing he was the only one laughing, stopped and actually looked kind of embarrassed.

I smiled. I was almost ten million percent sure Gabe was lying. As far as I could tell, everything he wore was black. Wow, though—he'd defended me.

"Thanks, Gabe," I said, and I meant it.

"Sure."

Frank shuffled his feet. He was weakened. It was time to banish him back to the shadow realm—that is, downstairs.

"Now what *are* you doing here, Frank?"

He held up a Tupperware container. "I just felt bad that you didn't get much dinner, so I brought you some dessert."

Now, when a brother arrives unbidden at your

doorstep with a slab of your mom's pecan pie, he quickly transforms from an enemy to your favorite brother. Still, he was standing between me and history. Well, me, Gabe and history.

"Thank you, Frank, my dearest," I said. "Now leave the pie and go."

He jerked a thumb back at the sign. "Anything to avoid being turned into a dead—and badly drawn—stick figure." He put down the pie and walked away. "Unicorn poop," he mumbled, desperate to fire off the last word.

I watched him go, then turned back to the door and bowed.

"May the ancient ones who guard the Monster's Castle—"

Gabe, to my surprise, finished the incantation: "Speed our safe passage through its halls."

My jaw dropped, and I stared at him silently for a good minute.

"Gabe, you do know the book!"

He shrugged. "It's awesome."

I just nodded, impressed. "Lead the way, fellow member of the Taylor legion."

We walked inside.

Gabe stopped and stared at the wall.

The pushpin over Alaska had fallen out and that

corner of the map had drooped, revealing the poster I'd drawn of my beloved vampire.

"Is that Lysander?"

My face went red. "Um, yeah. It needs work." I jumped on the desk and quickly covered up the poster again.

"No, it's pretty good. It's just that he wouldn't be holding that particular rose."

My eyes narrowed. "Are you saying I don't know my vampires?"

Gabe kicked at the ground. "No, it's just . . . uh, the rose you drew is a modern hybrid, and the one in the book is a blue rose."

My head swung around. "I *know* it's a blue rose in the book. It's called artistic license. Anyway, these blue roses . . . do they grow only in a specific location? Maybe Verona, New Jersey?"

"No. They don't grow anywhere."

"What?"

"The point about blue roses is that they don't exist in nature, but they're used all the time in poetry and operas and stuff. They represent unattainable or hidden love."

"So Rosaceae isn't a shortcut to finding a place name?"

"No. And it's pronounced more like rose-eh-she-ah. It's pretty basic Latin."

I threw a pillow at him. "Oh, *basic Latin.*"

He just let the pillow hit him and slumped his shoulders. "I didn't mean to be rude. I thought you might have been pronouncing it that way to test me. You know, like Cassandra does in chapter 2, when she questions Lysander's motives."

I was flabbergasted. I bowed to him, hand on my heart. "Gabe, thou hast out-referenced me. Now let's put these two great brains together and figure this out. Then you talk to your sister, and I'll convince my parents about the road trip."

"Sure."

"So," I said, "plants. You're an expert, obviously."

"Yeah, I like them." Gabe shrugged.

"You're being fake humble, dude. Admit it— you're good with plants."

He shrugged again but stayed silent.

He was squinting at the map, though.

"Climb on the desk, Lord Latin," I said.

"You sure? It's your desk."

"Oh, brother." I took my foot and cleared off the top, sending papers and books flying. "Look. Room for two. Move it."

He jumped up.

I gave a silent wish that the Jimi-constructed desk would hold our combined weight.

I pointed to the two Veronas, and Gabe nodded.

"I think that makes sense," he said. "You said that's where the play is set?"

"Yeah. Is there a Verona rose?"

"No." He paused for a few seconds, thinking. He actually scratched his chin like an old man with a beard.

I thought it was cute and chuckled. He was so lost in thought he didn't notice.

Eventually, he stopped scratching and stood up straight. "The weird thing about the Rosaceae reference in the poem is that it also says, 'Look where he fled, a blue Rosaceae sign.' So maybe it's not where Romeo and Juliet are *from* but where they *go*. Do they travel anywhere in the story?"

"Um, I'll be right back," I said.

A quick consult with Tom revealed that Gabe had hit the nail on the head.

"Romeo gets exiled to Mantua!" I yelled, bursting through the door. "Just like Lysander gets exiled to the United States!"

Gabe was so shocked, he almost fell off the desk.

I leapt up next to him. "Look for someplace called Mantua! You go east of the Mississippi and I'll look west."

A few minutes passed and then Gabe said, "Found it!"

He took the pushpin out of Verona, New Jersey, and placed it in the upper east corner of Ohio.

"Looks tiny," I said. You could barely make out the word "Mantua" on the map. "Nice eyesight!"

"Oh, I used this." He held up a small magnifying glass. Then he dropped his hand to his side and the glass disappeared.

For the first time, I noticed Gabe's pockets. There were, like, a hundred of them, and more zippers and pouches.

He saw me looking. "Always be prepared," he said. Reaching into another pocket, he pulled out a red marker and circled Mantua.

"You're, like, the biggest nerd ever," I said.

"I'm taking that as a compliment?"

"Zed calling you a nerd? That's my *highest* compliment," I assured him. "On to the next clue!" I pumped my fist in the air.

We moved on to the next stanza of Taylor's poem. It had a Latin phrase as well—*Et in Arcadia ego*—and the Gabe-approved translation was "There I also dwell." We got into a rhythm.

Gabe knew so much about plants and Latin that we'd soon transformed the ugly plaid pattern on my map into a stylish pocket square—that is to say, we'd corralled my chaotic mess of pushpins into something resembling a route that we could actually drive.

It started in Mantua, Ohio, and then went on to Arcadia, Indiana. Admittedly, from there, we were only *mostly* sure that the next stop would be Huzzah, Missouri. It could possibly be Marion, Illinois, but we figured we'd be able to get more specific directions after discovering the clues in the first two stops on the way.

After that, our options had us driving northwest or possibly southwest, but at least we had a direction to go: west . . . ish. Gabe and I shared a low-key fist bump (he refused a high five) on his way out the door.

The adventure was on!

Alone in my room, I danced my happy dance. The map was still pinned over Lysander, but he was partly visible. "I'll see you soon!" I whispered.

I couldn't see his mouth, but I knew he was smiling at me.

CHAPTER 8

Road Trip

I convinced my parents that I could go with Gabe and his sister; Gabe and I would fly home in a week, after helping Sam move in. Dad even got wistful as he told me about the road trips he and Mom went on before they had kids—probably just after the Cretaceous Period. I wasn't totally paying attention, actually. After he said yes, all I could think about was how to get Sam on board. As it turned out, I never had to use my charm on her.

Somehow, without my help, *Gabe* got Sam to agree to the trip.

And with just a week to go before summer ended, we were about to set off.

I posted a notice on the fan site telling the Taylor legion about our discovery. I didn't give all the details because to be one hundred percent honest, I wasn't sure about all the stops. But I did mention the first two, Mantua and Arcadia.

My fellow geeks had been unanimous in their praise.

GO FOR IT!

HELP LYSANDER AND YVES BE REUNITED!!!

KEEP US POSTED!!

I said I'd do my best to keep them all up to date from the road.

....

Finally, the day arrived. A special occasion such as this called for a special outfit. I had already planned to wear my bright purple sweater with funky squares all over it, but that morning, I also threw on my favorite white-and-black-striped sweatpants. I was ready.

Dad made me check for the thousandth time that I had packed my passport. I also had a letter of permission, signed by Mom the lawyer, letting Sam take me across the border.

Snacks? Check.

Other awesome sweaters? MANY! (Even in summer, fashion takes a front seat for this kid.)

Where were Sam and Gabe?

I heard the car before I saw it. Have you ever seen a nature documentary where a lion attacks a zebra, and the dying zebra makes this horrible noise?

That noise sounded like music compared to the clanking and wheezing that was coming from the next block.

I turned to Jimi. "You didn't happen to work on *this* car, did you?"

"Haha," he said.

The car made the turn. I'm not sure how it achieved that feat, but as it drew closer, I could see three different colors of paint, a dent in the front fender and what appeared to be duct tape holding the left headlight in place.

I immediately told the crowd my new nickname for the car: Rusty Raccoon.

"It's actually a 1996 Subaru Impreza," Jimi said.

"I'm not Impreza-ed," I said.

The car rumbled to a stop in front of the house. The driver's window rolled down and I finally met Sam. She had her head shaved on one side, and long pink-fringed hair cascaded down the other, partially obscuring a pair of green horned-rimmed glasses. She also had muscles on her muscles.

Sam turned her head slowly in my direction, like a demented doll.

"You're Zed?" It sounded like a challenge.

"Of course," I said proudly. "Nice car. Is it dead?"

Sam narrowed her eyes and spoke in a menacing voice. "It works fine."

"Really?" I pointed at the duct tape. "I've seen roadkill that looks more lively."

She scowled. "I could say the same thing about your sweater."

"Ah!" I gasped. "How dare—"

My mom coughed. "Thanks for agreeing to this, Sam." Apparently, she'd met Sam before and lived to tell about it.

"All good, Mrs. W.," Sam said. "Least I could do to say thanks for your help."

I had an instant picture of my mom getting Sam acquitted of some horribly violent crime. I made a mental note to tone down my witty comebacks.

Sam swiveled her head back toward me. "In the back. Front seat is for adults."

"Okay, then," I said.

Sam got out to grab my bags.

"How much luggage does one kid need?" she said, eyeing my suitcase, backpack and duffel bags.

"One must travel in style. A sweater for every occasion." I pointed to my current selection. "One of my best Value Village finds."

61

"What occasion is that for? A clown funeral?"

"Haha. I have an entire trunk filled with ugly Christmas sweaters."

"Please tell me you didn't pack those."

"It's August! Cottons only. What do you take me for?"

"You don't want to know. C'mon, sweaty. Move it."

SWEATY? I ignored that and hugged my family goodbye. They'd all woken up early to send me off.

Jimi handed me a box. "Might come in handy," he said. "Some walkie-talkies. I made a few adjustments."

The chances of the gift actually working were probably zero, but Jimi always had his heart in the right place. I hugged him. Then I slid across the worn fabric seat next to Gabe.

I don't know if it was being around his scary older sis full-time, but he seemed to have even less energy than Rusty Raccoon. He just kept staring out the window with his headphones on. Didn't wave or say hi. Well, that kind of behavior never stopped Zed Watson from trying to start a confab!

"Hey, good buddy," I said, giving him a friendly punch on the arm. He didn't respond.

I tried a different strategy. "Sooooo . . . road-trip snacks, amirite?" I reached into my backpack and pulled out three bags of goodies. "We've got Doritos — Cool Ranch, of course. These are stage-three snacks.

We'll save these until we've driven at least an hour—if this car doesn't blow up first."

I waved the bag in his face. No response. I grabbed another bag.

"Next, sourdough pretzels. These are stage-two snacks—can be opened soon after leaving your home city, but not right away."

Zippo movement from the human Eeyore.

Sam got into the driver's seat.

"Buckle up."

I did. Then I pulled out the *pièce de résistance,* a red cardboard box from the local coffee shop.

"Stage-one snack supreme. All good road trips must begin with the classic, a sour cream glazed donut. One eats this immediately upon pulling away from the house."

Sam revved up the engine. I put a donut and napkin carefully on Gabe's lap.

"Thanks," he mumbled. "But I'm not really into donuts." He passed it back.

I was shocked. Shocked! "Mary Motto #6," I said. "'Do NOT say no to a DoNUT.'"

But Gabe had gone back to staring out the window.

I was about to reach over and take off his headphones when I caught Sam shooting us a look in the rear-view mirror. Was Gabe scared of his sister? It was understandable. *I* was scared of her.

I pulled my hand back.

Then she gunned the engine and we drove away.

"We gotta make a pit stop," Sam said. "Pick up a couple of boxes."

Boxes?

"Pssst, Gabe. Your sister isn't a smuggler, is she?" The idea actually sent a thrill down my spine.

But Gabe said nothing. I thought he'd be at least a *little* bit excited. With Eeyore next to me and Darth Vader driving—this was not what I had hoped for.

I munched on my donut. "It's just you and me now, sour cream glaze," I grumbled under my breath.

· · · ·

"What's in these boxes?" I asked. "Rocks?" I heaved an eight-ton cardboard box into the trunk, being careful not to trap my own sweater-filled suitcase underneath.

"No spit, Sherlock," Sam said.

"I was kidding! These are seriously *rocks*?"

We'd stopped at a storage locker to grab the last of Sam's stuff. Not contraband, apparently.

At least Gabe was talking a little bit more.

"Sam studies geology," he said, helping me lift yet another box. "These are rock samples for her thesis."

"Geology is about rocks?! I thought it was, like, about weird stuff."

"What do you mean?"

"You know, like, 'Gee, that's a weird-looking dog.' *Gee*-ology."

Gabe giggled. I'd never heard him laugh before.

"Did you just giggle?" I asked.

Gabe stopped giggling. He stared at his shoes instead.

"Hurry up, you bozos," Sam said. "I want to hit the border before all the weekend shoppers are finished clipping their coupons."

We heaved the last box into the trunk and closed the lid.

Back in the car, I passed Gabe's untouched donut to Sam. She wolfed it down in one bite. Man, she was scary.

"Thanks," she said.

I saw her watching Gabe again in the mirror.

His headphones were once again clamped onto his head.

So far, this road trip had been about as much fun as the maiden voyage of the *Titanic*.

. . . .

About an hour away from the border, we hit a bump and I jolted awake. I must have dozed off. I immediately checked the clock on the dashboard.

11:53 a.m.

"Pretzel time!" I announced. I ripped open the bag and jammed a handful into my mouth. I offered some to Gabe, but he just stared silently out the window.

This had to stop.

I reached over and yanked one of the earpieces away from his ear. I'm not sure what he was listening to, but it was LOUD and there was even more screaming than back in the library.

He quickly fumbled with his player and muted it.

"What?!" he said.

"Pretzel time." I waved the open bag in front him.

To my surprise, he grabbed a few and began munching on them. That's when I noticed the plastic bin on his lap. He must have opened it while I was napping. Inside were some cucumber slices, several carrots and a beige-colored dip.

"Your parents sent you on a road trip . . . with VEGETABLES? What kind of parents do that?"

"Zed." Sam's voice from the front was sharp and stern.

Now, my social radar isn't always the best, but I know when someone is sending me "parent" signals, and this one was "shut up now."

I shut up.

For a few seconds anyway.

"So I made a playlist for the trip. Pre-border selections are mostly from the pop charts—banger bands from Korea, pop legends, and disco icons."

"Now we're finally talking the same language!" Sam said.

She passed me the aux cord, and I plugged in my player. (My "player" was actually an old smartphone that Jimi had "fixed" a few months before. Now useless as a phone, it was still great as a mobile music library.)

I hit Play.

"Karaoke time!"

Sam and I began belting out tunes.

Gabe wasn't joining in.

"Don't know the words?" I asked.

"Don't want to," he said, and he slipped his head-phones back over his ears.

Oh, well. At least Sam and I were sort-of bonding. Until she made me skip "Call Me Maybe"—an all-time best song!

"Seriously?"

"Just not my fave," she said.

I shook my head in silent disappointment and shock. We'd been doing so well.

And then we hit the border, and things got even worse. At least for me. All because of my passport.

Chapter 9

Border Cross

Here's the thing about my passport.

It, of course, has an awesome picture of my face. Well, as good as any passport picture can be when they won't let you flash your million-dollar smile or wear your funky glasses.

The problem is the bit that lists your gender and name.

My passport doesn't have my actual gender or my name.

It has my birth name and my assigned gender.

And this is the document I was going to have to hand to an already suspicious and grumpy border guard. How did I know the border guard was going to be suspicious and grumpy? Cross the US border some time.

It can be humiliating to have to answer questions based on information that's not about who you are.

I must have looked very anxious because Sam noticed and said, "It'll be over soon. And we have the letter from your mom, so everything's aboveboard."

Gabe even patted my shoulder. "This stuff makes me nervous too," he said.

I gave a weak smile.

What I didn't want to point out was that I wasn't anxious about crossing the border—I was worried about what I'd have to say and what someone looking at my passport might say to me.

Sam turned off the music. "Okay, quiet, guys! Or sorry, Zed? Is 'guys' okay?"

"It's all good. I'm a 'guys.'" At least she was trying to help smooth things.

Sam rolled down the window and made us get out our passports. I didn't want to show her mine, but she made me give it to her so she could pass it to the border agent. She didn't look at it. She simply held it in one hand and took out my mom's letter from the plastic sandwich bag I had stored it in.

"Passports, please," said the burly customs agent.

He had a beard and looked like he had laser vision that could X-ray anything just by looking at it.

I wanted to shut my eyes, but I was afraid that would make me look guilty or like I was hiding something.

The border agent took the passports without even a thank-you, which I thought was pretty rude. He looked at Sam's and Gabe's, and then at mine. "Which one of you is Zed?" he asked.

Except he didn't say "Zed" because that's not what's on my passport.

His mouth formed the other name as if in slow motion, and in my brain I was slo-mo yelling, "Nooooooo!"

But he had said it. Out loud.

There was an uncomfortable silence for a split second before Sam realized he was asking about me.

"In the back seat," she said.

"Yes." I gave a miserable little wave. "That's me."

The uncomfortable silence got longer. The guard stared at me, frowning. "And Zed is related to you how?" he asked Sam.

Except once again, he hadn't said "Zed"; he'd used a pronoun. And it was not the pronoun I used.

Sam grabbed my mom's letter. "I have a permission letter here from a parent." She passed it to the guard.

I wanted to sink into my seat.

The guard grunted and read the letter my mom had prepared.

Finally, after what seemed like an eon, he handed back the passports and waved us through.

"Speak up next time, Zed," he said to me as we passed. Except he hadn't said "Zed" that time either.

As soon as we were a couple of minutes into the US, Sam heaved a sigh of relief, rolled up the window and cranked the A/C. I swear the heat just across the border was about ten thousand times stickier.

Gabe looked sideways at me.

"Hey, Zed, how come your name is different than what the customs guy said?"

"It's my dead name—I hate being called that."

"But what were you, like, born as?"

I frowned and narrowed my eyes. "What were *you* born as?"

"Gabe? A boy named Gabe."

"Okay, but your name isn't Gabe. It's Gabriel, right?"

He nodded. "Yeah, that's true."

"So we all change and choose."

"And I'm Sam. Not Samantha or Samuel," Sam called from the front seat.

I could have hugged her.

"So I don't really need to tell anyone what I was born as. I'm Zed now. And that's what's important."

Gabe thought about this. Sam watched him in the rear-view mirror. "You okay with these questions, Zed?" she asked.

73

"It's cool," I said.

Gabe had more. "Okay, but what about when something like that border guard stuff happens? Why don't you correct people if your name is Zed now? Tell them that?"

"All my ID is under a different name. So when I go to the doctor or travel or whatever, people say the wrong name and use the wrong pronouns. So I try to keep it simple, as annoying as that is. Sometimes I just pretend I am that person, the one they think I am, and that makes it easier."

Gabe scratched his chin, so I knew he was still thinking.

I tried to come up with a good comparison. "Okay, you know how when Cassandra is trying to find out what happened to Marion Arbuthnot?" I said. "And she dresses up like a 'normal' person instead of a witch so she can walk into the Hall of Records?"

Gabe nodded. "She's trying to find out if there's any mention of where he went. So she's kind of acting like a human. It's a pretty funny scene, actually."

"Yeah, and sometimes it's like that for me—acting. I just put on my costume."

"That's cool."

"Haven't you ever wanted to put on a costume and pretend you're someone else?"

Gabe suddenly turned pink and mumbled something I couldn't hear. Then he put his headphones on and went back to looking out the window.

"Humph," I said. I turned my attention back to Sam. "Zed requires disco."

Sam shook her head. "Nope. It's time for some old-school rap."

I sighed. "I'm in more of an electro mood."

"Aw, Zed! This is *exactly* the sort of music you need to pump you up after crossing the border."

She put on a song I'd never heard before. It opened with this awesome beat, but then the singing started and the lyrics were . . . well . . .

"Are you sure this is appropriate for kids?" I asked.

"My car, my rules."

"Okay." I shrugged.

"Besides, Zed Watson, isn't it great?"

"Heck yes," I said, dancing in my seat.

Sam didn't hear me, though, because she'd turned up the music and was singing along.

The quest was back on track.

Soon, Sam and I were shaking Rusty Raccoon with our moves.

Maybe we shook it a little too much, though, because just as we got on the highway, disaster struck.

The A/C made a grating noise like the sound of a bunch of tiny plastic bits getting stuck in a vacuum, and then—silence.

"Did . . . did the A/C just stop working?" I asked.

Sam smacked the vent nearest to her with her hand and said a word from the song.

"I'm not sure that's appropriate either," I said as the air started to get hotter and hotter. "Are we losing oxygen?"

She ignored me and continued to hit the dashboard.

"I'm melting!" I said.

Sam pounded and pounded, but the A/C refused to rise from the dead.

"Dang it!" she said finally. She slumped back, defeated, then rolled down the windows.

"The outside air is even hotter!" I yelled.

"Cut it out, Zed," Sam growled.

"I have to tell you I don't appreciate your tone, and also, I will literally, actually die without air-conditioning. Just so you know."

She rolled her eyes at me in the rear-view mirror.

I decided to take this to a higher power. "A/C gods, DON'T GIVE UP ON US NOW!"

"Why are you yelling?" Gabe asked. More screaming poured out of his headphones.

The car was now boiling hot and incredibly loud.

"All right!" said Sam. "Yes, the air-conditioning died. We're just going to have to deal."

"This stinks!" I yelled. "This whole road trip stinks. No one likes my snacks. You won't play my

music. I just got misgendered, and now I'm going to die of heatstroke!"

"You're going to die of something," Sam said in a slightly threatening tone.

I ignored her. "And I'll never find this stupid manuscript and learn what happens to Lysander and Yves, and nothing will ever be good again!"

Gabe actually groaned. "Calm down, Zed," he said.

"Are you serious?!" I stuck out my tongue.

"Zed is sticking their tongue out at me!"

"Gabe is being mean!"

"Am not!"

"Are too!"

Sam pounded on the steering wheel and the horn blared.

"That's it!" she said through gritted teeth. She drove onto the shoulder and slammed on the brakes.

"Uh-oh," Gabe whispered. He started to put his headphones back on.

Sam's head spun around. Her eyes flashed red.

Gabe froze.

His sister looked demented. "Stop. Talking. Don't. Move." She took a deep breath between each word.

"Now, I am only going to say four words: Shut. Up. Ice. Cream."

"I'm pretty sure 'ice cream' is one word," I said.

"It isn't!" she yelled. "And if I hear one more word out of either of you, I'm going to turn this car around and dump you over Niagara Falls. Do you understand?"

We nodded silently.

Sam put the car in gear, and we drove back onto the highway. After a minute, she turned the rap music back on.

I leaned over to Gabe, lifted one of his earphones and whispered as quietly as I could, "Why did she say 'ice cream'?"

CHAPTER 10

Ice Cream

After a half hour of silent (except for rap on repeat) driving, we rolled up to the dinkiest little ice cream place you've ever seen. It was basically a shack off the highway in the middle of a gravel parking lot. A handmade sign said Local Diary instead of Local Dairy, which made me laugh.

"Do you think they serve pencil-flavored ice cream?" I joked.

"No," Sam said.

Gabe still had his headphones on, so he didn't laugh either.

Sam parked the car and got out, immediately yanking the back door open on Gabe's side.

She started whirling her arms in a circular motion. "All right, you chuckle-heads—outta the vehicle. C'mon, let's go! *On y va*. Move your butts!"

Gabe was moving slower than a sleeping sloth, so I climbed over him and leapt out.

"What are you doing?" Sam asked.

What I was doing was limbering up my arms by making chopping motions through the air with my hands.

"Take that, evil vine!" I said, cutting through the imaginary enchanted forest surrounding and hiding the Monster's Castle.

"Take a chill pill," Sam said.

I ignored her. Then, to wake up my lower half, I started doing the twist.

"When I said 'move your butts,' that's *not* what I was thinking of." She made a face. "I must avert my eyes."

"Ha!" I said. "I have to remain limber and practice my mashing skills."

"Your what now?"

"Mashing. You know, like the 'Monster Mash.'" I put on my best Dracula impression. "'Whatever happened to my Transylvania twist?'"

"Points for creative thinking," Sam said, rolling her eyes.

"The 'Monster Mash'! You know? The song?"

"I've been listening to that song since before you were born, weirdo."

"Weirdo?" I fake gasped and clutched my chest.

"Now, come on—ice cream awaits!" She said this in her own Dracula voice, which was awful.

"That was awful," I said.

"Just for that, no sprinkles."

"Ah!" I gave a mock shriek of horror.

By this time, Gabe had finally moved his butt out of the car, so together we made our way over to the menu board.

No pencil flavor, BTW. But a ton of choices.

What to choose?

What to choose?

Gabe lowered his headphones and went up to the window first. I was too engrossed in the possibilities to notice what he ordered.

Sam ordered too, apparently, because the woman at the window started waving at me to get my attention.

"Hey there! You ready to order, young man?"

Young man.

I frowned. She wasn't being mean, but it still stung. As I'd told Gabe, though, this happens all the time, so I'd learned some techniques to help deal with it. Sometimes I pretended I was an undercover detective, which was fun. But this time, I conjured up an image of myself slapping away mosquitos that were buzzing and saying "she" and "he" and "what's your real name?"

That made me feel better.

My mom called these daydreams "Zed moments." She'd be talking to me, and suddenly I'd get distracted by something funny or interesting in my brain.

"Having a Zed moment?" she'd ask, and I'd shake it off and tell her what I was thinking about.

The ice cream lady didn't say, "Having a Zed moment?" But she did call out in a louder voice, "Hello? Can I help you with anything?"

I was jolted back into the real world.

And my eyes locked on the perfect Zed selection.

"What is that?" Gabe asked as I turned around with my triple-scoop cone with sprinkles (no matter what Sam had said).

"It's Cookie Monster." I took a dramatic first lick. "Yummy and perfect."

"Perfect?"

"For me. Because (a) cookies, (b) monsters, (c) ice cream and (d) all of the above!"

I took another lick. It was maybe the most delicious thing I'd ever eaten.

"It's turned your tongue *bright blue*!" Gabe laughed.

I noticed his cup of what looked like a lump of oatmeal. "What flavor did you order?" I asked. "Glue?"

"It's banana," he said.

"Since when is banana grey?" I asked.

"It's a 'naturally occurring' flavor."

"That's an insult to the time-honored tradition of both ice cream and the United States of America, land of spray cheese and supersized soda."

"It's actually *more* authentic," said Gabe, brightening. "The yellow coloring in the banana ice cream you get at grocery stores is fake."

"You mean delicious," I said. "I notice your ice cream doesn't do anything cool to your tongue."

Gabe ignored me. "I mean, think about it—is the inside of a banana yellow? No, it's more like this whitish color." He pointed to his cup and grinned.

"Okay, but think about this!" I said. "What's a more *fun* ice cream experience? Eating a delicious bright yellow thing that sort of tastes like banana? Or eating a weird beige-white-gray thing that maybe tastes *a little more* like banana? I rest my case."

"Whatever," Gabe said. He shrugged and went back to eating his ice cream—out of a cup, mind you. I mean, really.

"What's the point of eating it if you can't just lick it until your tongue turns blue?" I sighed and shook my head.

I went to sit on the picnic bench where Sam was enjoying her giant waffle cone of birthday cake ice cream. A choice I could get behind.

But she was frowning.

"Sam, how can you be eating sunshine and happiness in a cone and be frowning?"

"I'm not," she said. "I don't have sunglasses, so I'm squinting. Appreciate the nuance, Zed."

"Point taken." I, of course, was now sporting my own star-shaped (prescription) sunglasses.

Sam took another lick, and this time she did frown. "Plus, I've had better cake flavor, TBH."

My jaw dropped. "TBH? Did you just use text-speak IRL? Whoa."

"I did, Zed. You may think I'm uncool, but actually I'm *super down* with the kids. I *get* the *lingo*. I'm so *hip* with it." With her free hand, she snapped her fingers, then made a finger gun and pointed it at me.

I had to admit, Sam was pretty funny when she wasn't being absolutely terrifying.

"Sam, you're pretty funny when you're not being absolutely terrifying."

"And you're surprised?"

"Impressed." I gave a slight nod of my head in appreciation.

The ice cream was working its magic.

But I was growing antsy about getting back on the trail. We hadn't even arrived at our first stop, Mantua, and we were already taking breaks. The ice cream did help with the heat, though.

As soon as I crunched the final bit of cone, the heat seemed to return with a vengeance.

I looked over at Gabe.

He was kneeling down right in the middle of the parking lot. He had set his empty ice cream cup and spoon down next to him.

"What the?" I said to Sam, pointing at Gabe.

"Hmmm," Sam said.

I squinted.

I could make out the tiniest, scrubbiest little cluster of flowers in front of him. They seemed to be wilting in the heat.

Gabe was smiling at them.

Then he pulled a tiny bottle from his pants pocket, unscrewed it and poured its contents onto the flowers.

"Gabe is so weird," I said. "I mean, as a fellow weirdo, I respect weirdness in others. But I don't get the point of carrying the world's teeniest flask of water around just to pour it on some weeds. To each their own, I guess."

Sam didn't say anything, but she wiped her hands on her pants, stood up and went over to Gabe.

She knelt down next to him.

A whole family of weirdos, I thought. Sitting down on a parking lot is uncomfortable—there are tiny rocks and pebbles that poke your butt and thighs. Kneeling must have been even worse.

Gabe pointed to the flowers, and Sam smiled, then she put her arm around him. I felt a lump in my throat.

Suddenly, I missed my family and my house. I wanted to show my sister Mary my blue tongue and have her wrinkle her nose and say I was gross. I had an image of the big tree in the front yard that helped keep the house cool.

Sam's voice drifted over to me. "While I'm away . . ."

I snapped out of my Zed moment. I could hear Sam and Gabe talking quietly across the parking lot. I wasn't sure if they knew I could hear them, so I tried my best not to listen, but I did catch some things.

"But Dad doesn't get it," Gabe said.

"He has a hard time letting you know he gets it, but he does. I promise. You just have to tell him when he's wrong."

"It's hard, though," Gabe said.

I picked at the white paint that was peeling from the worn wood of the picnic table.

Sam gave Gabe's shoulder a squeeze. "I know! But he is trying. I told him what you and I talked about the other day, and he's going to back off the soccer thing."

"Really? But I had to promise to play or he wouldn't let me go on this trip."

"I talked to him. He didn't realize you were so unhappy."

I thought about why Gabe had been in such a funk so far. Maybe it was because of this?

"I don't want to hurt his feelings. I know he really wants me to play."

"He already *has* a kid who loves sports." She pointed to herself. "*Moi!* You love different stuff. He'll come around. Okay?" she said, lightly patting his back.

"Okay," Gabe agreed.

I felt bad for listening in, so before they could say anything more, I clapped my hands together and leapt off the bench. They both looked over in surprise.

"All right, folks!" I said. "On to Romeo exile!"

Sam stood and extended her hand so Gabe could pull himself up. So Gabe hated sports and Sam had to stick up for him. I could picture that, but it made me bummed. I resolved then and there to pay better attention when Gabe talked about stuff he was interested in, like plants and flowers—and not just in *The Monster's Castle*. I bounded over to them, reinvigorated and ready to be on the road again.

"Friends, Romans, Romeos, Gabes and Sams, on we go!"

Sam laughed. "You know, Zed, you're pretty funny when you're not being absolutely melodramatic."

"It's true. I'm a very flamboyant and well-regarded drama kwing."

"Drama what?" Gabe asked.

"Kwing. It's a combo of 'queen' and 'king,' for us theydies and gentlethems."

"Are you still speaking English?" Gabe asked.

"Never, Gabe. I speak Zed."

"You know what? That tracks," Sam said, laughing, and she ushered us into the car.

We were finally back on our way to Mantua!

CHAPTER 11

Mantua

Of course, we still had hours of driving left with no A/C.

The summer heat poured through the windows as we left New York and started cutting across Pennsylvania. Pleading and begging got Gabe and me two more stops for ice cream. Well, one for ice cream and one for lunch, with ice cream for dessert.

At one shop, the woman called me "little girl." At the other, "sonny."

As we drove on, I began regretting the choice I'd made at the second shop.

Bubble gum ice cream is like Hawaiian pizza.

If it's good, it's fine.

If it's bad, it's horrible.

Still, I wasn't letting it go to waste as Sam announced, "Road sign says Mantua is ten miles away."

"It's pronounced Man-ah-way," I said.

Gabe shook his head. "That makes no sense at all."

"I looked it up before we left."

I stared into the rear-view mirror and opened my mouth wide. "What color is my tongue?"

"Same as your lips," Sam said. "Blue. Like a corpse."

I grinned. "Perfect."

....

We drove into downtown Mantua.

Actually, we didn't. Or more precisely, we couldn't.

The entire Main Street had been blocked off by cars.

"Oh no," Gabe whispered. "What happened?"

"It's fine," Sam said quickly. "See?" She pointed to a giant banner that stretched across the road.

MANTUA POTATO STOMP FESTIVAL

"I can see the need for a potato *chip* festival," I said. "But a street party for plain old spuds?"

Gabe, on the other hand, was suddenly super-stoked. "Oh! I wonder if they have any new varieties?!"

Sam and I exchanged a look in the mirror. We grinned.

Sam parked on the shoulder of the road, and Gabe shot out the door.

"Remind me again why we're here?" Sam asked, turning around.

I adopted my best Hollywood tour guide voice.

"If you look out your windows, you'll see the first real stop on our Zed and Gabe Adventure Tour is the tiny potato-loving town of Mantua."

"Got it. But Man-uh-*why*?"

"Nice wordplay."

"Thanks."

"Taylor's poem mentions Shakespeare's lovers. Romeo, as we now know, fled to Mantua. The poem also points to roses, skulls and angels."

"Graveyard images."

"Exactly! Which is a sign that the poem links to the first chapter that Taylor left behind, 'The Vampire's Grave.' Here's a taste."

I pulled out my notebook and, before Sam could protest, started reading:

Lysander St. Clair woke in the dark. But not the dark of his own coffin—no, this was a darkness that pressed in and choked him. A darkness

91

that seemed alive. He moved his slender hands around and felt . . . dirt. Lysander was trapped underground. What had happened to him?

Then it came back in a flash—how his new hiding place had been found out. How those who had sent him away from his beloved home had tracked him down, across oceans and continents and into the deep forest.

They had dug a grave and pushed him into it. They'd expected him to die.

Well, they had failed. He allowed himself a small smile. He was awake, and he was going to find Yves. He thought again of the howl that had pierced the night sky on his journey to America.

And Lysander knew in his heart that Yves would try to find him as well, and together they would escape this exile.

"We will return to the Monster's Castle and live together forever, Rosaceae and orchids and everything in full bloom all year round—a testament to our undying love."

I closed the notebook with a flourish.

"See? The chapter also mentions that Latin rose thingy, so we're operating on the assumption that we're looking for a grave or a graveyard or a gravestone here in Mantua."

"And it might even have a rose near it, on it or over it?" Sam asked.

"You get the idea perfectly."

"Okay. Now, any idea *why* you're looking for all that stuff?"

I hesitated. "Well, we're not totally sure yet. We're kind of hoping that finding the clue will explain that."

"Remind me again why I agreed to this?" she said. "Never mind. It's because I'm a doofus. Speaking of doofuses, I'd better go find my bro."

We set off down Main Street, where the whole town seemed to have gathered. Vendor carts lined the sidewalks and were packed with bushel baskets full of potato seedlings and cuttings. There were artists selling paintings of potatoes. There was even somebody walking around dressed like a potato, playing a fiddle.

"It's spud-tacular!" Gabe said. He was like a kid in a potato store.

A moss-covered stone wall stood at the far end of the street.

"The graveyard is over there," I said, pulling him away from a cart filled with—guess what?—potatoes!

"I'll get us some snacks," Sam said. I was pretty sure I knew what was on the menu in this town.

Gabe and I marched away down the street. As we passed through the cemetery gates, the fiddle music grew fainter and fainter.

We began to move slowly among the graves.

There were more than I expected. About five John Smiths. A few Mary O'Reillys. But nobody named Lysander. And no St. Clair.

"No vampires, as far as I can tell," I said.

"How would you even know?" Gabe asked.

"Oh, I'd know," I said confidently.

The sun blazed as we eliminated more graves from our search.

"Whew, it's hot."

"Maybe take off the sweater?" Gabe suggested.

"Never!"

He shook his head and kept walking.

"This is taking too long," I said eventually. "We need to speed things up. If I were a vampire's grave, where would I be hiding? I need to think like a corpse."

I grabbed some dandelions and lay down on the nearest grave.

"I'm dead. I'm dead. I'm dead," I intoned. "Oh, where can my bones rest in peace? Oh, woe. Oh, woe."

"Oh, brother." Gabe rested his head on the gravestone. "Can we take a break and look at some potatoes?"

"I can't answer that. I'm dead."

"Fine. You stay here and decompose. I'll go look at some more graves."

"Oh, woe is me," I said.

He was still looking and I was still decomposing when Sam's face suddenly loomed over top of me.

"If you're dead, it leaves more room for me and the Gabester in the car."

"Hardy har har. Any luck finding snacks? Are they all potatoes?"

"Yes and no. I scouted a good food truck parked near the stage. Pizza and sandwiches, and of course, fries."

"Potatoes at their truest selves, IMO. I can't be dead if I'm craving fries this much." I got up and carefully laid the dandelions on top of the grave. "Let's go."

Sam waved at Gabe. "Break time!"

I looked at him hopefully. "Any luck?"

"Nope."

"Me neither." I hoped the fries would help revive my declining spirits.

And in a way, they did.

Chapter 12

Monster Mashed Potatoes

The picnic tables were all set up on a large field near a tent-covered stage.

The speakers were blaring some country tunes, and the field was filled with people eating, chatting and even dancing.

I'll say this for the potato party animals: they knew how to have a good time.

They also knew how to prep taters. The Mediterranean fries in particular were amazing! Lightly salted, with a hint of cumin.

They momentarily took my mind off the futile search for the grave.

Maybe it wasn't a grave we were supposed to be looking for? Maybe we got it all wrong? I pushed that horrible thought out of my mind.

"This town sure does love taters," Sam said with a snort. She polished off her pizza. "I'm going to see if there's anything else worth looking at."

"Me too!" Gabe jammed a final handful of fries into his mouth and stood up. "You coming, Zed?"

"I'm good," I said. "The only potatoes I'm interested in are deep-fried and sitting in front of me."

"Okay. Hey, are those Idaho reds over there?!" He was off.

More farmers were pulling up in dusty trucks, unloading huge crates of produce—not just taters but corn, beans, tomatoes as red as a vampire's breakfast. There were also ribs being prepped on a long wooden table with smoking grills behind it.

It looked like they were getting ready for a good old-fashioned BBQ.

I spotted Sam by a booth with some tie-dyed T-shirts. A sign said the dyes were "All natural. Made from taters." No sweaters that I could see. Not worth getting up for.

Gabe was now by the trucks and had struck up a conversation with a group of farmers. They were excitedly passing around some potatoes and stuff. Boring.

Then, just as I was noshing on my third serving of (excellent) fries, the walking potato walked up to the microphone.

The country music suddenly stopped.

"It's the moment you've all been waiting fooooooooor," said the spud, his voice rising with each word. "The Potato Dance-Off!"

I stopped mid-chew, entranced, as six more people

in potato costumes rushed out on stage. There was a huge cheer from the crowd, and people began forming a kind of mosh pit. Maybe a "mash" pit?

The potatoes counted down: "3, 2, 1!" Then music came blaring over the loudspeakers.

And do you know what song they played?

"Mashed Potato Time" by Dee Dee Sharp!! This is one of those golden-oldie songs from before technology and fun existed. There's even a dance that goes with it. Mom Watson loves that retro stuff, and she taught all of us kids this dance before we were out of diapers.

I was up like a shot, pushing my way to the front of the lawn.

I twisted my heels, waved my arms, wiggled my butt. Oh, my goodness, it felt amazing!

"C'mon, everyone. Let's cut a rug!" yelled the potatoes.

Some ninety-year-old grandma joined me. Pretty soon, about a dozen of us had formed a mashed-potato conga line. A circle closed around us, townsfolk and farmers clapping along with the song.

I spotted Gabe and Sam staring from the crowd, eyes wide.

I bowed to them and gave one last jiggle of my backside as the song ended.

I let out a howl, "POTATOOOOOOOOO-OOOOOOOO!!!" And me and Grandma hugged.

The spectators and the potatoes gave a huge cheer.

Next thing I knew, the biggest spud was handing me a giant potato-shaped purple ribbon! AND IT MATCHED MY SWEATER!

"This was a contest?" I said.

"You were the bee's knees," Grandma replied.

"You too!" We hugged again.

I pinned the ribbon on my sweater and accepted the high fives and slaps on the back.

"Next up, the 'Monster Mash'!" yelled the potatoes.

I think I squealed so loud the tent ripped.

I started dancing, but soon Gabe tapped my shoulder. "I've got news," he said, smiling.

"You found the grave?"

"Maybe. I was talking to those farmers, and it turns out the graveyard we were looking in is the new graveyard."

"New? Those dead people were, like, ancient."

Gabe shrugged. "The town has been around awhile."

"And?"

He leaned in close. "There's a secret older grave-yard hidden in the woods!"

My eyes bulged. "Let's go!"

But I admit that I cast a sad glance back at the dancing potatoes as we hurried away.

· · · ·

The woods were amazing. Creepy. Vines hung down from trees. The path was almost completely over-grown, and we practically had to cut our way through the bushes and branches. It was like each tree had hands that reached out to stop us from moving forward.

"OMG!! This is so perfect!" I said.

But that was nothing compared to the graveyard itself. If a vampire was ever going to rise up from the ground and chomp into your jugular, it would happen in this graveyard.

Everything was covered in yellow-green moss (*Sematophyllum demissum*, according to Gabe). Strands of other green stuff hung off the branches of the knotted ancient trees. You could barely see the gravestones underneath years' worth of decaying branches and leaves.

And it smelled amazing. Wild roses grew almost everywhere.

"OMG, it's MORE PERFECT!" I yelled.

Gabe brushed aside some vines from a slab of stone.

"Julius Bramble. Aged 22 years. 1776–1798," he read. "Isn't that a name from the book?"

"It's one of the baddies who buried Lysander." I shoved aside some branches covering a large stone. There were a bunch of names. "James Skinner. Mary Skinner. Abraham Skinner. All of them are also baddies in the book."

"This is definitely the place!" Gabe said.

I could imagine Taylor sitting right there, breathing in the scent and the atmosphere. Then starting to write.

But where was Lysander?

We began rushing from stone to stone.

Finally we found it, almost lost in the twisting roots of an enormous willow tree. A large carved stone urn, cracked and mossy, peeked out from atop a mass of thorny rose vines.

"There must be a gravestone under that!" I said.

Gabe got down on his knees and used both hands to make a window in the vines. "Bingo. And there's a rose carved on the stone." He peered in closer. "There's some blue pigment left. It's a blue rose!"

We started pulling at the vines. They fought back, scratching and clawing at our hands.

"Whoa!" Gabe and I said together.

We stood up and took a step back.

Lysander St. Clair
Aged 33.

We had found it.
The Vampire's Grave.
Gabe hugged me. "It's all real," he said.
I started to cry. Tears of joy.
"Wow. We're on the right track." I wiped my eyes and nose on my sleeve.
Then I stopped.
"Weird," I said.
"What?"
"I've seen a lot of gravestones in my research. And the inscription on this one is weird."
Gabe saw it too. "Oh, yeah. It just says 'Aged 33.'"
I walked over and pointed at Mary Skinner's grave.

Mary Skinner
1778–1832
Died Aged 54

"But Lysander's doesn't say 'died.' It just says 'aged,'" I pointed out.
"And it doesn't have dates," Gabe said. He stooped down and started looking more closely. He knelt and began running his hands over the stone. "And this is also weird. There's lichen all over the front and inside the numbers. But the dot hardly has any."

LYSANDER
STCLAIR
AGED 33.

"What dot?"

"This is a dot here, right after the 33."

Now I knelt down. "Maybe a bullet hole?"

"Maybe." He ran his finger over the edges. "It's pretty smooth, though."

"Maybe there are other marks?"

We cleared away all the brush around the grave. There were no more secret markings. The lid of the carved urn didn't come off.

"I guess the clue has something to do with this weird inscription on the front," Gabe said.

"We should take pictures!"

I swung off my backpack and pulled out an instant camera I'd "borrowed" from my brother Tom.

Gabe pulled a digital camera out of some hidden pocket in his pants and took a close-up.

"Good thinking," I said. "Yours will be way higher res. Of course, mine will be more artistic."

"Sure," Gabe said. "One last question: What the heck does this clue mean?"

I gave a deep sigh. "I have no idea."

CHAPTER 13

Putting Camp in Camping

"Lysander St. Clair."

"Aged 33."

"Lysander St. Clair."

"Aged 33."

"Lysander St. Clair."

"Aged—"

"Can you two stop saying that over and over again?!" Sam said.

We were back in Rusty on our way to a campground not far from town.

"But we have to figure this clue out!" I said. "Lysander St. Clair."

"Aged 33."

"STOP IT NOW OR I WILL DUMP YOU TWO ON THE SIDE OF THE ROAD."

"And my mother the lawyer will be in touch," I countered. "Aged 33."

"Lysander St. Clair."

"Fine!" Sam said. "Look, once we get the camp

set up, I'll help you figure this out. But please give me some peace until then. It's been a long day."

"And an awesome one," I said.

Gabe and I fist-bumped. But we whispered the clue to each other the rest of the drive.

One other good thing happened, which is that Sam was able to find a gas station that could do a quick fix on the A/C! Turned out there was just a leak in a hose.

So we enjoyed the cool air again as we drove toward the campsite.

Finally, Sam pulled into the entrance of some state park. WoodWood or TreeTree or something like that. There were a lot of trees.

Gabe started jumping around like a puppy. "Look at all the ferns!"

"Down, boy," I said.

"I wonder what else grows in the woods?"

Sam offered a few suggestions. "Wolves. Grizzly bears. Venomous snakes."

"You're joking, right?" I asked nervously.

"Oh, Sam," Gabe said, "the snakes here aren't venomous."

"You mean there *are* snakes?!" I started looking nervously at every shadow in the trees.

Sam grinned at me in the mirror. "It's okay. If one gets in your sleeping bag, catch it. I know how to cook them."

"You two are bonkers," I said.

. . . .

The campsite itself was actually kind of cozy.

At least, I was cozy.

Sam lit a fire and set up some chairs.

I had, of course, packed a few blankets from home. Frankenstein, Wolfman and the Creature from the Black Lagoon were wrapped around me as I watched the sparks float in the air.

I was also watching Sam set up the tents.

Gabe had disappeared into the woods the second we'd parked.

Apparently, camping involves sleeping on the dirt in a flimsy piece of fabric stretched around some metal poles.

Who knew?

Sam grunted and hammered in the pegs to anchor the first tent into the ground. "Anyone going to help me?" she asked.

I sipped my iced tea.

"Sam," I said, sticking out my pinky while I held the straw and slurped the refreshing drink, "you're always talking about how buff you are. Sun's out, guns out, right?"

She grunted.

"So in my view, you should see this as an opportunity to show off your athletic *prowess*." I emphasized the last word to sound smart and fancy. Taylor was always writing about the monster's "athletic prowess," so I assumed it was a compliment.

Sam laughed a hollow laugh. "You're really a pain in the butt, you know that?"

"It's all part of my Zedly charm," I said, and blew bubbles into my tea.

....

Gabe reappeared just as Sam finished setting up the second tent.

"Nice timing," I said. "Like showing up in the kitchen after the dishes are done."

"You have got to be kidding me!" Sam cried.

"What?" I yelped. "I was here for moral support."

Beaming from ear to ear, Gabe was covered in mud, sticks, dirt and who knew what else. Well, he probably did.

"You wouldn't believe how much poison ivy is in these woods!" He smiled.

Now Sam and I shared a look.

"Dinner," Sam announced. "And, Zed, you're doing the dishes."

Over dinner, we took a closer look at the photos Gabe and I had taken. But we still couldn't figure out what the heck the grave was trying to tell us. Even Sam just shrugged and said, "Yep. That's weird."

She did let me borrow her phone, though, to do a quick update on the quest for the fan site. I had to stand on top of the car to get a signal, but I was able to fire off a quick post about the grave. I even added a photo, in case anyone else could help us figure out the clue.

There were more messages of support, saying things like "MONSTERS UNITE!" And "REVEAL THE TRUTH!"

And one weird one, from a new member of the site with a handle I didn't recognize: @Hi_Its_Another. Their message simply said, "How are you sure this is the right path?"

I was about to answer when Sam yelled, "Don't use up all my data."

I turned off the phone and jumped down from the car.

The sun set.

The fire crackled.

"We don't have the clue figured out," I said, "but at least it's marshmallow-roasting time! Right?"

Sam nodded, looking even more demented in the reflection of the glowing embers. "You can roast two each. Then bedtime."

"Two!" I said. "After all the dishes I washed? This is child labor!"

"Two or zero," Sam said.

"She means it," Gabe whispered.

"Fine." I roasted and ate two marshmallows. Of course, I also ate a ton more unroasted marshmallows. It's not like Sam told me I couldn't do that.

CHAPTER 14

Weirdos

Sam let Gabe and me each take a mug of hot chocolate to bed in our tent.

"First night of camping, we always get some kind of treat," Gabe explained. He downed his quickly.

I, on the other hand, like to savor.

"Cool. Where do I plug in my mug warmer?" I looked around the tent but couldn't find an outlet.

Gabe snorted. "You really aren't much of a camper, are you?"

"Camp—that I get. Camp-ING? Don't see the attraction. So you're saying there is no outlet?"

"Good night, Zed." He flicked off his battery-powered light.

I sipped my chocolate in the darkness.

The absolute darkness.

The darker-than-my-windowless-closet-of-a-room darkness.

And since there wasn't an outlet, there was also no way to plug in my night-light.

Even with the three pillows I'd brought, plus the extra comforter and slippers, I found it impossible to sleep.

It wasn't just the roots and stones and sticks jabbing me in the butt.

It was the noise. Nature is not quiet.

There was a rustle in the trees. It sounded huge.

I heard a wolf howl. It sounded hungry.

Was that a snake slithering?

Then a roar just a foot away from my head!

"Gabe, wake up! WAKE UP!"

"I wasn't asleep, Zed. We've only been here, like, two minutes."

"I hear a bear," I said.

Gabe chuckled. "That's Sam snoring."

"Seriously? I might need to borrow your earphones."

Gabe chuckled again.

"I'm not kidding," I said. "They help you block stuff out, don't they?" I hadn't meant it to be mean or anything, but Gabe stopped chuckling.

I heard him turn over. "Good night, Zed."

"Sorry, Gabe," I said quietly.

He didn't say anything.

I tried to settle myself down. I focused on the cool ground and pretended I was a vampire sleeping in an open grave. Of course, that got my mind working on the actual grave we'd found. So sleep? Not happening.

I was about to ask Gabe if he was still awake when I heard him whisper, "Zed? Are you still awake?"

"I don't know how I could be asleep with all these rocks in my backside," I whispered back.

It was dark, but I could hear the rustle of fabric while Gabe readjusted himself.

"You get used to it eventually," he said.

"Do you camp often?"

"Yeah, Sam, Dad and I go camping a lot in the summer. Sometimes even in winter."

"Well, without a mug warmer, you can count me out for that. I can't imagine intentionally doing this more than once a decade."

His voice seemed to get quieter. "It's one of the few things my dad and I both like."

There was a short silence, then a click. Gabe had switched on the camping lantern, and it flickered for a second before coming on fully with a low humming noise. He was propped up on one elbow, staring into the light.

I sat up, rearranging my pillows to support my new position. Gabe reached into the pocket of his pants and pulled out a folded piece of paper.

He unfurled it in front of us. It was a copy of our map.

Man, this guy and pockets.

"I didn't know you made a copy," I said. I admired his neat handwriting and the notes around each place name, as well as the question marks he'd added for some of the other possible destinations.

He ran his hand over the paper to smooth its creases. "Are you worried we aren't doing this right? What if we're completely wrong or can't figure out all the clues?"

"Nah, we'll figure it out, Gabe. We've already got this far. The grave exists! We were right about that, and we'll be right about the rest. We're smart cookies," I said, borrowing a phrase from my dad.

I didn't mention the question from @Hi_Its_Another. They hadn't said we were on the *wrong* path. It nagged at me a bit, but I wasn't sure why.

Gabe smiled at me. "How do you do that?"

"Do what?" I'd been having a Zed moment.

"Stay so positive all the time. Like nothing bothers you."

I thought about what he was saying. But I knew it wasn't true. I remembered the times today—and the many times before—when I had been misgendered, called a little girl or boy. I'd felt awful.

"But I am bothered," I said. "All the time."

"You never show it." Gabe looked down at the

116

map. His hair completely covered his eyes, so I couldn't see his expression.

"I mean, c'mon, Gabe, you have to admit I did kinda lose it about Rusty Raccoon's A/C breaking down this morning."

"Rusty Raccoon?"

"That's my secret nickname for Sam's car."

He smiled. "I saw the end of you losing it, but how did that all start?"

"Oh, you had your headphones on, so maybe you didn't hear that?" I thought back to what I'd said earlier about Gabe blocking things out. He wore his headphones almost constantly. And he was so quiet.

I thought he might turn off the light, but he surprised me by carrying on the conversation.

"It's kind of like a superpower, being positive like you."

"Um . . . maybe. I do try. I told you I sometimes pretend I'm in disguise."

"Like Cassandra pretending to be human."

"Yeah. It's one of the reasons I'm so into *The Monster's Castle*. It helps me try to stay positive, because the monsters are so positive. They help me accept my inner monster."

Gabe thought about this. "Maybe me too, in a way."

"Inner monster? You?" I thought of how careful he was to step around weeds and bugs every time we stopped the car.

"Well, how do you mean it?" Gabe asked.

"I just mean that reading the book, or what we have of it, helps me accept that I'm never going to be 'normal,' or un-weird."

"Like how the monsters in the book refuse to change when the humans want them to be un-weird."

"Exactly. Taylor clearly makes the monsters the heroes. And that means being weird is okay. Better than okay, actually."

"But what if, when we find the rest of the book, we find out the monsters do give in?"

"No way. Think about how awesome they are in the chapters we have. They're only going to get more awesome."

Gabe sat thinking.

I did too.

He broke the silence. "So for me, being weird is being really into plants. Which is, I guess, a little weird."

"Yeah," I said. "And for me, it's understanding that I'm not cis."

"Cis?"

"Cisgender. It means you are the gender you were born with."

"Got it. But you're *not* cis?"

"Right. I knew that my assigned gender wasn't me."

"You said you're nonbinary."

"Yes. Which, for me, means I don't actually identify with a gender. He, she, girl, boy—neither feels like me."

"So they/them," Gabe said.

"And even with a great family like mine, there are challenges in coming out as nonbinary. People can think it's weird. And they don't always understand me."

"Like ice cream sellers constantly calling you 'little boy' or 'little girl.'"

"You noticed that?"

"Yeah. The last one kept saying 'she' even after Sam called you 'they' twice."

"Yeah, that happens all the time. But reading *The Monster's Castle* helps me realize that it's not my problem—it's theirs. That's why I'm so drawn to the monsters. The monsters don't let how people see them affect how they see themselves."

Gabe smiled. "And that lets the monsters stay positive. So they never give up on their weird quests. Lysander and Yves, and Marion and Cassandra, don't stop trying to be together and don't stop searching for each other. Well, at least in the chapters we have."

"Positively correct," I said. "Taylor got that accepting your inner monster is amazing." I held up my cold mug of cocoa. "To Taylor."

Gabe held up the lamp. "To Taylor."

We clinked.

"TO BED!" Sam called from the other tent.

Gabe smirked and shut off the lamp. "We resume our quest tomorrow!" he said in a whisper.

"Confident in who we are," I said. "A couple of weirdos."

"Good night, Zed."

"Gabe? Thanks for noticing the ice cream thing."

"No problem. I even noticed that it's 3–2 for boy versus girl."

"Seriously?"

"Yup."

"That is hilarious. You should write down the tally in one of your notepads. Ooh, we could even make a game out of it."

"Game?"

"Yeah. We'll predict what we think each server will call me. If we disagree, it's a bet. Loser buys the ice cream."

"Sure. That sounds like fun."

And in just seconds, he was snoring.

I lay back on my pillows and tried to fall asleep by repeating the mantra in my head.

"Lysander St. Clair."

"Aged 33."

"Lysander St. Clair."

"Aged 33."

"Lysander . . ."

CHAPTER 15

Arcadia

Of course, my saying the mantra all night didn't get us closer to solving what it actually meant.

But that didn't stop our momentum.

"Okay, monster hunters," Sam called from the front seat of the car. "Almost in Arcadia. It's time for our daily recap. Why are we heading here?"

I cleared my throat and began. "The third stanza in Taylor's poem is from the point of view of a bat."

Gabe chimed in. "And the bat talks about a *memento mori*."

"I thought it was someone's name. But of course it's Latin."

"It means 'a reminder of death.'"

"That's creepy," Sam said. "So why aren't we looking for someplace called Memento or Mori?"

"If I may continue," I continued. "The poem links to the chapter called 'The Witch's Familiar.'"

"Let me guess," Sam said. "The familiar is a bat?"

"I *knew* you were a secret fan of the book!" I said. "The witch is named Cassandra Gray, and she is awesome. She flies around at night kicking butt and casting spells on people who have wronged her and her monster friends." I started making "piew piew piew" noises, so Gabe picked up the story.

"Cassandra wears a charm that her zombie friend made for her, and it has the words '*Et in Arcadia ego*' carved on it."

I pulled out my notebook and read a selection, doing my best to sound like an awesome-cool English witch.

As Cassandra flew over New York, she spied Marion running through the rain-soaked alleyways. His own battalion was in hot pursuit, guns at the ready. He was unarmed, having denounced the tools of violence that had made him a soldier. A soldier for a cause he no longer believed in.

"Marion, run!" Cassandra called. But her voice was swallowed up by the fog and gloom.

"Traitor," they had called him.

"Hero" and "friend" were the words she chose.

There was a shot, and Marion fell.

Cassandra's rage knew no bounds.

Marion had once saved Cassandra on the battlefield.

Now she had to save him.

Another shot rang out as the witch hurtled toward earth, her broom nearly breaking apart with the speed.

As she reached the rooftops, the soldiers looked up, their eyes wide with horror.

In a flash she was upon them, kicking, slashing, casting spells.

In seconds, she had defeated them all. They lay unconscious at her feet.

BEEP! BEEP! BEEEP!

All of a sudden, Sam's phone beeped loudly.

"Uh, you wanna answer that?" I said.

"Finish the story!"

Ooh! She was gripped.

I resumed the narration.

"Cassandra," said a weak voice.

A mere glance at Marion showed Cassandra that she was too late. Life was leaving him.

"I will save you," she said.

"No. I know what that will do to you. My life is not worth that."

"It's my choice." She closed her eyes and laid her hands on his wound.

Lightning flashed as Cassandra spoke the words that would transfer the last of her sun magic to him. The magic flowed from her fingertips.

Was the cost too great?

Cassandra saved Marion, knowing that doing so sentenced them to never-ending separation.

Marion now rises at dawn to wander the world alone. Each night, he must die again.

With only her moon magic remaining, Cassandra must escape the sun's rays or she too will die.

For only a fleeting moment, at dawn and sunset, can they dare to exchange a greeting before each must flee to safety.

Now Cassandra has only her beloved familiar to ease her loneliness.

She holds up the memento mori *Marion left for her one day in her belfry home.*

She gazes at it when she misses him and reads the words: "Et in Arcadia ego."

"It's all so creepily Gothic I could just die!" I said.
"*Et in Arcadia ego* means 'There I also dwell,'" Gabe said. "When you jam the Latin and the translation together, you get 'I live in Arcadia.'"

BEEP! BEEP! BEEEP!

Sam still ignored the phone.

I cut in. "Anyway, to make a short story long, Taylor is telling us to look for a church in the town of Arcadia, Indiana, because the bat and Cassandra 'dwell' in the tower of an abandoned church during the daylight hours."

"We think the clue must be hidden somewhere up in the belfry," Gabe said.

BEEP! BEEP! BEEEP!

Sam tossed her phone back to me. "Figure out why it's making that noise."

I picked up the beeping phone off the seat next to me and read the screen.

"There's a text. It says, 'Alert. Tornado warning. Morgan County. 9 a.m. to noon.'" I looked outside. Dark clouds were gathering around us. "OMG!!! That's here!" I yelled.

"That's now!" Gabe said.

At that precise moment, the skies opened up.

The wind howled.

A bolt of lightning struck a telephone pole just as we drove past it. The thunder shook the car.

Gabe and I hugged and prepared for the worst.

"I think I hear a tornado!" Gabe yelled.

"We're all going to diiiiiiiiie!" I yelled.

"If you two don't calm down right now, a tornado will be the least of your worries," Sam said.

Rain began to pour down like someone had turned a hose on our windshield.

Sam cursed under her breath as the storm intensified. She hit the hazard lights and clutched the steering wheel so tightly her knuckles turned white.

Gabe and I kept hugging. I'm not sure who was shaking more.

Then another flash of lightning illuminated—

"A bell tower! Over there!" I yelled, pointing toward the church.

Sam swerved, and we sped off the road and onto a soaking wet gravel parking lot. The tires spun as the car slid across the slick stones.

Lightning struck the bell tower, sending electric blue spikes down to the ground.

And that revealed a low stone wall.

"We're headed right for it!" I yelled.

Sam slammed on the brakes. They squealed, and the car began to rumble and bounce. Then we stopped. I could see the stone wall just outside my door.

"And that's how a boss parks a car," Sam said. She turned off the engine.

The double doors of the church swung slightly in the wind about twenty feet away.

"Let's make a run for it," Sam said. "It's just a little rain."

Little rain? Who was she, Thor?

"Can't we get closer first?" I asked.

The wind roared, and I'm pretty sure I saw a tree and a cow flying past us. Why was nature always out to get me?

"Forget running," I said. "Staying in the car has got to be way safer."

"I don't think you know how tornados work," Sam said. "This is the *worst* place to be right now."

"I'll take my chances." I looked out at the driving rain. "Maybe you've noticed that your brother and I are not wearing bathing suits."

"I'm not either, doofus." Sam pointed at the church. "We're heading there—*now*." Rummaging around on the floor, she found an old newspaper. She spread it over her head and opened her door. "Follow me on three."

She got out.

"One . . ."

Gabe started to open his door, but that was hard with me grabbing on to him for dear life. The rain was joined by pellets of hail.

"Two . . ."

The rain fell harder.

I shook my head. "We are never—"

"THREE!"

Sam sped away and disappeared through the doors.

I was still holding on to Gabe.

"I just saved your life, Gabe. And my sweater."

"It's *just* rain," he said.

"It's a TYPHOON!"

"We have an umbrella." Gabe reached under the seat in front of him and pulled out something that might once have been a working umbrella but now resembled a mangled spider.

"It looks like something Jimi tried to fix," I said.

"It'll keep us dry." He opened his door all the way.

"Are you bonkers?" I asked. "An umbrella attracts lightning."

"Um, no. Science." Gabe stepped outside and opened it up. It had so many holes, it stopped precisely zero percent of the driving rain.

"You look like a demented Mary Poppins."

A bolt of lightning streaked across the sky.

Gabe shrieked, tossed the umbrella to the ground and leapt back into the car, soaked completely through.

"Next great idea?" he said, shivering.

Before I could answer, there was a loud thump on his window.

"AHHH!"

Gabe and I jumped.

A shadow filled the window.

"The angel of death," I whispered. "I knew it!"

Then a face appeared. A kindly woman smiled.

"I'm Darlene Stamford," she said, cupping a hand around her mouth to be heard through the door.

Gabe opened the window a crack.

"I'm the minister here. Your sister suggested you might need some help?"

Darlene was wearing a dark suit and a white collar. The shadow we'd seen was an enormous umbrella. It appeared to have steel girders helping it withstand the wind.

Darlene noticed me eyeing the contraption. "Yes, we do get some very epic storms around here. Helps to be prepared. Your sister came and found me. I told her to wait inside. C'mon, let's get you two some hot chocolate."

Magic words.

The wind died down. The rain seemed to lessen. The lightning and thunder moved farther away. Birds tweeted.

Gabe and I poured out of the car and under the wide berth of Darlene's umbrella.

To tell the truth, the rain was still beating down pretty hard.

We hustled toward the church. The spire rose so high it seemed to be lost in the low clouds. The rain made the old stone slick and glossy, like a giant candle.

"It's a beautiful old church," I said.

"Mm-hmm. And much drier inside than in your old car!" She let out a loud throaty laugh. I liked her instantly. "But you're right—built just after the town was settled, about two hundred years ago or so. But the bell is the real beauty."

Gabe and I exchanged looks.

"The bell?"

"Mm-hmm. It was made just after the Civil War. Out of melted-down bullets and cannonballs. That's a powerful image of peace, if you ask me." She lifted her head. "They shall beat their swords into plowshares . . . And nation shall not lift up sword against nation, neither shall they learn war anymore. Amen."

As we approached the doors, I looked down and saw two deep grooves filled with water. Tire tracks. But there were no other cars in the parking lot.

We walked inside.

Sam was sitting by a warm radiator, sipping a cup of tea. She had a large blanket wrapped around her.

"Your hair looks like wet snakes," I said.

"You're lucky Darlene is a better human being than I am," Sam said, then sneezed. "I'd have left you in the car until tomorrow."

I pretended to be offended. Darlene had already told us that Sam had asked for her help.

"You are a monster," I said.

"From you, that's a compliment. But next time I tell you to run, RUN!"

I pinched my sweater sleeve and smiled. "And yet, I'm safe and bone dry."

She scowled and sneezed again. "I notice you let my little brother take the brunt of the storm."

Gabe looked down at the pool of water that had formed around his sneakers. "Good for flowers, good for me," he said with his patented shrug.

Sam decided her tea was more interesting than this conversation and turned away.

"The storm warning is still on for a little bit," Darlene said. "But the worst does seem to have passed."

A ray of light even shined through a window, sending a beam of gold across the floor.

"Before the hot chocolate, can we have a look at the bell tower?" I asked Darlene.

She got a strange look on her face. "Wow! Three months with barely a visitor, and now two people on the same day wanna see our bell."

CHAPTER 16

In the Belfry

A chill ran down my spine. I thought of the tire tracks I'd seen in the parking lot.

"Two people?" Gabe asked.

Darlene nodded. "A historian from some college out east. Said he was researching bells and wars and stuff. He was here a few hours ago. Left right before the storm."

I calmed down a bit. It was just a coincidence, bad timing. But I knew enough about monster stories to know that you still had to be on guard in case a coincidence was something more.

Darlene led us over to a set of stairs. A red-velvet rope was strung across with the words "Do not enter" written on a handmade sign. She unclipped one side.

"The steps take you to the level under the bell. There's a ladder and a trapdoor you gotta lift for that last little bit."

"Thanks!" Gabe and I said in unison.

We hurried up the stairs.

Darlene called after us, but we were running so hard we couldn't hear her over the pounding of our feet.

"What did she say?" I asked Gabe.

"I think she said something about the storm starting again soon."

"We'd better be quick, then."

Turns out there are a lot of stairs in a two-hundred-year-old bell tower. And the ladder was about a gazillion feet high.

"Footprints," I said, noting a few in the dust around the bottom of the ladder.

"Size twelve or so. Our historian is pretty tall."

I climbed up first and stuck my head through the trapdoor.

A few pigeons squawked and flew out between the slats in the arched windows as I pulled myself up.

Gabe joined me. The floor was thick wooden planks covered in dust and bird poop. Spiderwebs floated gently in the breeze.

"No bats, though," I said with a sad sigh.

The bell was suspended above us, out of reach. It was big and beautiful. We could read the inscription engraved along the rim. It was the same Bible quote that Darlene had recited in the parking lot.

Gabe took a couple of pictures.

"Think the quote might be the clue?" he asked.

"It doesn't really match anything from the fragments." I thought back to the grave we'd seen in

Mantua. "There were numbers on Lysander's head-stone. Anything like that?"

Gabe and I walked around the bell.

"I don't see anything," he said.

"Maybe inside the bell?"

We stared up into the dark bowl.

"I *think* I see something? Maybe?" Gabe said.

I looked around for a way to get up for a closer look.

There was a stepladder folded up and leaning against one wall. I grabbed it and set it up under the bell. It rocked slightly on the uneven floorboards.

"If I stand on the bottom rung and you balance on the top rung, I think we can reach inside the bell," I said.

"Why do *I* have to get on the top rung?"

"Well, what if there's an inscription inside, but it's in Latin?"

Gabe thought for a second. "Fine. But you better hold on to me tight."

He stepped up carefully. He had to stand on tip-toes to get his head into the bell.

I stood on the bottom rung and hugged his knees.

"Just need a second to adjust to the light," he said.

"You're heavier than you look," I said.

"It's my enormous brain."

"Haha. See, Gabe? You can be funny. It's rare, like a blood moon, but it happens."

"Wait. I see something." He stretched a little higher and pushed the heavy metal clapper to the side.

"Oh," he sounded disappointed. "It's not numbers. It says . . . 'Big Blue.'"

"Big Blue?"

"Yeah. Maybe a reference to blue roses?"

"Seems like a bit of a stretch. I can't think of any mention of 'Big Blue' in the fragments. Still, we'll make a note of it."

"Okay. Let's go," Gabe said.

But before we could move, there was a loud whirr from just above us.

"What the—"

The bell began to vibrate, then swing.

Gabe grabbed the lip of the bell for balance and

was swung violently to the left. I strained to hold on. If I let go, Gabe would fly through the air.

The ladder teetered underneath me. But then the bell swung back, and we settled again.

"Let go!" I said.

"Okay!" Gabe said.

I looked up.

"DUCK!" I yelled.

Gabe hunched down just as the clapper swung by his head and slammed into the side of the bell.

BOONNNNGGGGGGG!

The sound was deafening.

The bell began to swing the other way, knocking us to the right.

This time, the ladder tipped over. Gabe fell on me and we both fell to the ground just as the bell tolled again.

BOONNNNGGGGGGG!

We scrambled to our feet, covered with dust, and practically jumped back down through the hatch.

We ran down the ladder and the stairs. The bell continued to ring, shaking the steps beneath our feet.

When we got back to the nave, Sam and Darlene weren't there. The church doors were open, and light poured in.

We ran outside. They were both staring up at the tower. I assumed they were worried about us.

BOONNNNGGGGGGG!

"I never tire of that sound," Darlene said.

"It is beautiful," Sam agreed.

The sound echoed off the nearby trees.

"Beautiful?" I said, panting for breath, my ears ringing. "You mean deadly!"

"That bell tried to kill us!" Gabe yelled.

Darlene looked at us, confused. "I said to remember that it's almost noon."

"I thought you said 'soon,'" Gabe said.

"Or 'loon'?" I suggested.

Darlene started to laugh so hard she nearly doubled over.

Sam narrowed her eyes. "Did you just say the bell tried to kill you? How?"

"The clapper almost knocked my head off!" Gabe said.

Sam looked amazed. "Are you telling me you had your head inside a giant metal bell?"

Before Gabe could answer, Sam marched toward him fast. I was about to yell "Run!" when she reached out her arms and hugged him.

"You are a bonehead," she said.

"I'm so sorry," Darlene said. "I didn't even consider that you kids would do something like that."

Sam glared at me. "This has Zed written all over it. Darlene, is there a train station nearby with trains back to Canada? Or Siberia?"

I gasped.

"Don't blame Zed. We both thought it was a good idea," Gabe said.

"Well, it was a stupid idea." Without warning, Sam came over and hugged me too! "Apparently, I need to keep a closer eye on you two." She let me go.

"Thanks," I said. I gave a sheepish smile.

Sam heaved a sigh. "Well, there's good news: we found the clue."

Gabe and I were totally flustered.

"How do you know about Big Blue?" I asked.

"Big Blue?" Darlene said. "But that's just the name of the bell."

Sam chuckled. "There's a plaque outside the stairs you went up that tells you that."

Darlene nodded. "Didn't need to look inside a bell to find that out."

Sam put a hand on my shoulder. "I meant that *we* found the clue—Darlene and me. See, we started talking and . . . well." She pointed up at the side of the church tower, right over the doors we'd just run through.

Carved into the stone was a gargoyle. A BAT gargoyle. And it was clearly pointing at numbers.

1284

"What are those?" I asked.

Darlene smiled. "1284 North Cassandra Street. That's the address for the church. Well, the old address, before the town made some changes a few years back. If you look online, we're at 35 East Avenue now."

"Cassandra Street!" Gabe and I said together. "So the address is the clue."

Gabe pulled up the photo of Lysander's grave. "We've got lots of numbers now. 1284 and 33. Or maybe 33 dot."

"Dot?" Darlene asked.

"Yeah," Gabe said. "The grave said 'Aged 33.' But there was a dot after the 33."

"We thought it might have been a mistake—or, like, maybe a bullet hole or something. Because it was newer than the numbers."

"How do you know?" Darlene asked.

"Lichen," Gabe said. "It's an organism that grows on old stones, and it was all over this one, except inside the dot. Which means someone added the dot much later."

"So the dot might be significant," I said. "But we don't know for sure."

"Let me see that picture," Sam said. She looked at

the photo and then back up at the gargoyle. Her face broke into a wide smile.

"Thank you, Professor Burns," she said. She handed back the camera.

"Who's Professor Burns?"

"My geology prof. She takes us out each term for a geocaching tournament. And thanks to the dot, I think what we have here is a coordinate: 33 *point* 1284."

"So we know where the treasure is!" Gabe and I were practically jumping up and down.

Sam held up her hands. "Whoa, whoa, whoa! Hold your horses. We have one possible coordinate. Probably latitude, if we're looking in the right part of the planet. So, 33.1284 north. You need both longitude and latitude to figure out an exact location."

That only lowered our spirits a tiny bit. We could feel the thrill of the chase. We were on the right track!

That's when I noticed them: large footprints in the gravel. But Darlene said the historian had left before the storm. Were these new prints or old ones that had filled with rain?

I was about to take a closer look when there was a clap of thunder and the skies opened again.

"Storm's back," Darlene said.

"Back into the church!" Sam yelled.

I might still have stayed to examine the prints, except a fleeing Darlene yelled, "And I have ice cream to go with that hot chocolate!"

CHAPTER 17

Huzzah!

I wanted to update the fan site with the exciting news, but the campground outside Arcadia was too remote and Sam's phone just refused to connect.

I figured I'd try the next day and just enjoy the camping.

Well, not the camping so much, but definitely the veggie stew and celebratory s'mores for dinner.

Gabe and I, of course, had trouble sleeping. We could feel in our toes how close we were getting.

"Tomorrow we hit Huzzah, Missouri," I said.

"Then we'll have almost all the clues," Gabe said, slightly louder.

"Nothing can stop us now!" I practically yelled.

This was followed by an even louder "BE QUIET" from Sam's nearby tent.

So we stayed quiet, and eventually we fell asleep under sparkling stars, with visions of vampires and campfires dancing in our heads.

Not that everything was blue roses and sunshine when we did get back on the road.

The stretch of highway after Arcadia wasn't what you'd call exciting.

Gabe and I tried and failed to play I spy.

"Wheat."

"More wheat."

"Corn."

"More corn."

"Sky."

"More sky."

Sam finally ordered us to quit, but we did get an ice cream pit stop out of it.

Cherry sprinkle bomb with a side order of "Would you like that in a waffle cone, little boy?"

Then it was back in the car with nothing to do but feel impatient.

So I decided to pass the time by edumacating Gabe about good music.

"I made a playlist," I said.

Gabe groaned. "You already made me listen to your playlist when we started out, remember?"

"(A) You didn't listen. (B) That was standard stuff. I made a *secret* playlist for when we started actually finding the clues. Ready?"

"No." Gabe reached into his backpack for his own headphones.

"Sorry, Gabe. I grabbed them while you were brushing your teeth this morning."

He slumped back in his seat. "Please no more Beyoncé."

"Ha! Only a couple of her tunes. But I did some research, and we start off with something I'm sure you'll love."

I clicked Play.

The unmistakable sound of a heavy-metal guitar riff blasted from the speakers. It was soon joined by some driving drums and then a primal scream.

Not my cup of tea, but some palatable Metallica. I could live with it as long as it was followed by some of my fave bangers.

I smiled at Gabe, who looked like a bird had just pooped on his head.

"What?" I said. "It's Metallica! Every metalhead loves Metallica!"

"Who the heck is Metallica?"

Sam started laughing in the front seat.

"What's going on?" I asked.

"Hand Gabe his player and the aux cord," she said.

I reached into my backpack and grabbed Gabe's stuff.

He plugged in his player.

The loud shrieking I'd heard in snippets came through the speakers, but instead of driving guitars, the singer was backed up by violins, trumpets and cellos.

She stopped shrieking, then began singing something in . . . Italian, maybe?

"Wait," I said. "You. Like. OPERA?"

"No. I *love* opera. Haven't you noticed my shirts?"

I looked at the one he was wearing. "It says you like butterflies."

"That's *Madama Butterfly*. It's an opera by Puccini."

"And yesterday you had on a shirt with a barber pole. I figured you liked haircuts."

"It's from *The Barber of Seville*!"

I blinked.

"By Rossini!"

I blinked again.

"Wagner? The *Ring* cycle shirt I wore on Monday?"

"I thought that was for *The Lord of the Rings*."

Gabe shook his head sadly. Sam just started laughing again.

"Gabe, you never cease to amaze me," I said.

"Thanks."

"So what opera is this?"

"*Aida*."

"Eye-eater? Still sounds like a heavy metal band to me."

GABE AND A NEW FRIEND

"*Aida.* A-i-d-a. It's Verdi's masterpiece. Although the libretto was written by Ghislanzoni. My fave."

A light bulb went off. "Flora and Aida."

"FlorAida." He nodded. "My username on the site."

The music swelled. Sam joined Gabe in some high-pitched singing.

"This music is horrible," I said.

Gabe handed me his headphones.

. . . .

About seventeen million hours later, the opera finally ended and I was able to take off the headphones.

"Are we done torturing cats?" I said.

Gabe sighed. "Culture is lost on some people."

"What a very Zeddish thing to say," I said.

"So what the heck is a huzzah?" Sam asked as we headed across the Missouri state line.

"It's a word that British soldiers used to cry to get pumped up for battle."

"HUZZAH!" Gabe yelled.

"Geez!" Sam swerved slightly, then straightened out the car. "Do. Not. Do. That. Again." She took a deep breath. "More explanation, please, Zed."

When someone asks Zed Watson for an explanation, I oblige.

"Marion Arbuthnot is the name of Taylor's revenant monster—or zombie, as they're more generally called. He says 'Huzzah' in a chapter called 'The Revenant's Chest.'"

"Okay. Following so far."

Gabe, lover of words, jumped in. "The title is actually a double pun because Arbuthnot has a chest where he hides his letters from Cassandra. But he also got shot in the chest."

"He was killed by his own troops after he 'betrayed' them at the Battle of Bunker Hill. It wasn't really a betrayal, though, because they were horrible people. He says at one point, 'Is a cause for war just if the warriors are unjust?'"

"Legit Q," said Sam.

"That was another controversial part of the book. In the chapter we have, Taylor portrayed the colonial soldiers as cruel and bloodthirsty. Marion was more of a pacifist."

"Then—bang!—they shot him," Gabe said.

I sighed. "But as you know, Cassandra saved him. Sort of. Now each one can only leave letters for the other to read. I'll give you a sample of one of them."

I gave a quick cough and recited the relevant part of the chapter from memory:

Oh, Cassandra!

I despair that we shall never talk face to face again. I wander the world by day, hunted and hunting.

My only solace is the words you write to me at night and leave for me to find when I wake.

I know these delicate papers will fade and decay as I await some miracle that unites us again. But the words will never leave my mind or heart.

I utter a feeble "Huzzah" for a dream that someday we may again be allowed to meet.

Yours forever,

M.

I wiped a tear from my eye. "And we won't know if they ever meet again until we find the rest of the book."

Sam did not seem moved. "So the dead dude says this word, and that's got us stopping in some dusty heck-hole looking for what exactly?"

Gabe perked up. "Well, thanks to you, now we know we're looking for coordinates, so it *has* to be a number. Maybe a street address like the church?"

Sam snorted. "So are we hoping to find a Zombie Avenue in Huzzah?"

We didn't say anything.

She shot us a look in the rear-view mirror. "How much of this journey is just you two making stuff up?"

"We're two for two so far," I said, "making stuff up."

"And after Huzzah?"

"We'll cross that bridge when we come to it."

"We're looking for a bridge?" Sam asked.

"It was a metaphor," I said.

"Yeah," Gabe agreed. "And maybe there *is* a Zombie Avenue in Huzzah."

"Well, you can look it up on my phone. We have to stop for gas." She pulled off the road.

"Sam, I don't feel you have quite entered into the spirit of this journey," I said.

She pointed at the clock radio on the dashboard. "Ticktock. May I remind you that this is *my* journey? And I agreed to these side trips as long as they weren't too far off the highway."

"And so far, we're right on time," Gabe pointed out.

Sam snorted. "With only two near-death experiences, inside a tornado and a bell. I can't wait to see what disasters lie ahead with you two."

"The likeliest disaster I can see is that the A/C breaks down again," I said.

Sam turned off the ignition. "I've got to get this stuff to my dorm room and get ready for classes in four days. If we find this weird little kiddie comic book of yours before that, cool. If not, you help me unload and get on a plane back home—without the book."

Even though she had said this in a calm voice, it was one of the scariest things I'd heard from her on the entire trip.

CHAPTER 18

Wish You Were Here

Turned out there was an ice cream stand inside the gas station.

I'd predicted the old dude would call me a boy.

Gabe had said girl.

One full tank of gas and a pink twinkle swirl cone and chocolate dip later, we were back inside Rusty Raccoon.

But I was bummed. First off, the old dude in the gas station had handed me the cone with a smile and an "Enjoy it, little girl." Which meant the ice cream was on me.

Gabe brought me up to date on the running score.

"Boy 5, girl 5!"

"Anyone use 'they'? Or even 'kid'?" I asked miserably.

He pretended to check the list. "Um, no. Well, unless you count Darlene. But she knew ahead of time."

"Hmph. Predictable."

The second thing that had me bummed was that a quick check on Sam's phone had turned up no zombie-themed or even zombie- or monster-adjacent places in Huzzah.

And Sam had ordered us back in the car before I'd had time to check on the fan site.

We drove into town, if you can call it that.

There was only Main Street. About twenty old wooden buildings leaned at odd angles. Some had their windows boarded up. A number of front doors were gone, making the buildings look like they were twisted faces with missing front teeth.

Everything seemed covered in a layer of reddish dust.

"Looks like a perfect home for a zombie," Gabe said. "Or a ghost."

I was starting to love him.

Sam let out a loud whistle. "Looks more like one of those ghost towns you see in old Westerns."

She parked the car in front of a low brick building. It seemed to be the only one with glass left in the windows. Even those were covered in iron bars.

We got out.

A faded sign over the door read United States Post Office.

"Who gets mail here?" Sam said. "Tumbleweeds?"

"I bet the post office would know if there was ever a Zombie Street," Gabe said.

"Or maybe somebody named Marion Arbuthnot?"

"I don't think anybody's been named that for two hundred years," Sam said. "At least not by choice."

A warm breeze ruffled my hair.

Actual tumbleweeds rolled down the street.

"This is hopeless," Sam said.

I thought about the post office again. "Marion's always getting letters from Cassandra. Maybe this is where we need to look?"

"Is it open?" Gabe asked.

The windows were covered with so much dust it was impossible to tell if there were lights on inside.

"Only one way to find out," Sam said. "Actually, *you* two find out. I'm going to walk around and see if the ghosts offer anything for lunch."

She did not seem optimistic about this as she turned and walked down the street. The middle of the street, actually, because there were no other cars anywhere in sight.

"I hope we meet again, dear witch!" I called in my best Marion Arbuthnot voice.

She waved her hand over her shoulder and kept walking.

I turned back around.

Where was Gabe?

"Gabe!" I called. "Have you been kidnapped by a ghost? You have all the luck."

"He went into the post office, doofus," Sam called.

"Oh." I pushed the rusted metal door, and it creaked open. How had I missed that awesome sound?

The air inside was actually cooler. It smelled like flowers, and the walls were lined with dozens of wooden mail slots. Almost all of them were empty, but they were also polished and dusted. They gleamed in the soft light of the post office lamps.

The inside was as clean as a whistle, as my mom likes to say. She'd never said that about my room, of course, but I'd heard her mention it about other places in our house.

Gabe was standing in front of a long wooden counter.

He was already having an animated conversation with a guy who looked as old as the town. He wore a name tag that said "Jerry."

". . . first post office in Missouri!" Jerry was saying. "We've been in operation since the town was founded in the 1800s."

"And still going since the town ended, by the looks of it," I said. I waited for a laugh.

Jerry frowned at me. "City slicker, huh?"

"Sorry. It just seems like the town has—"

"Yes, yes. Fallen on hard times. A lot of small towns have these days." He gave a deep sigh. "But you should have seen us back in the day."

"The 1820s?" I joked.

This time he gave me a grin. "No. Back when I was a little younger, this was even a bit of a hangout for all sorts of interesting people. Good times." He stopped talking and just kind of stared out the window for a minute.

"I think he's having a Zed moment," I whispered to Gabe.

"What do you mean by interesting?" Gabe asked.

Jerry shook his head like he was waking up from a dream. "Yeah. Musicians. Writers. Painters. Creative types. There was a kind of annual meet-up every Fourth of July. It was a real humdinger."

He looked like he was about to start staring out the window again, so I quickly jumped in. "You've lived here a long time, then?"

"All my life."

Perfect.

"Any chance there's a street or maybe a building with the word 'zombie' in the name?" I asked.

"Nope."

"No Zombie Street?"

"Nope."

"Zombie Zone?"

"Nope."

"Revenant Lane? Dead Guy Gulch? Poltergeist Boulevard? Ghost Cul-de-Sac?"

"Nope, nope, nope and nope."

My shoulders sagged. Were we wrong about Huzzah?

Gabe tried a different tack.

"How about Arbuthnot?"

Jerry grinned. "Now *that's* interesting."

"It is?" I asked. "How?"

Jerry winked at me. "Sometimes you have to ask the right questions to find the answers you're looking for."

He ducked down behind the counter and popped back up again holding a metal box. He flipped open the lid and began pulling out postcards.

"This is the strangest thing. No one by the name of Marion Arbuthnot has ever lived here."

"We never said his first name," I said.

"I *know*!" Jerry was really grooving now. "But someone has been sending postcards to a Marion Arbuthnot every year for the past forty years."

"Forty years!"

"Yup. Started up and never stopped."

He laid the postcards on the counter. They covered the entire area. They all had pictures of odd places: Salem, Massachusetts; Loch Ness in Scotland; Edgar Allan Poe's grave in Baltimore; the Banff Springs Hotel in Alberta.

"This person has good taste," I said.

Jerry smiled and turned one over.

"Every year, a postcard from someone named General Wolf has arrived here in Huzzah. It's always prepaid, so there's no return address or postmark. And here's an even stranger thing."

"What?" Gabe and I asked together.

"No one called Arbuthnot has ever lived here—or even, as far as I can tell, visited here."

Gabe and I leaned over the cards. Each one had the exact same line handwritten on the back:

When you are ready, come dine with me.
Signed,
General Wolf

And they all had the same address:

Marion Arbuthnot
PO Box 107
Huzzah, MO

"Who owns box 107?" I asked. Could Taylor secretly be living here in Huzzah? Were we that close?

Jerry laughed. "No one does. It doesn't exist."

"What?" Gabe and I said.

"There are barely a hundred people who remember this town *exists*, let alone live here now." He pointed at the wall behind him. It was full of shiny gray metal boxes with locks and numbers on tiny brass plates.

"The numbers end at 74," Gabe said.

"Yup."

"So why keep the postcards?" I asked.

"Because it's one of the most interesting things that has ever happened in this job. It's a mystery!"

"You got that right," I said.

"Can we have one?" Gabe asked. "To help us solve this mystery?"

"I don't see the harm in that after all these years. Which one do you want?"

Gabe pointed at one with a Venus flytrap at the exact same moment I pointed at one with a haunted Transylvanian castle.

"Why not one each?" Jerry said with a huge grin.

We beamed.

"Jerry, thank you so much."

"It was a pleasure serving two such amiable young kids."

I turned to Gabe. "So 107 is the clue! Let's grab Sam's phone so we can figure out the coordinates." We started to give each other a high five.

But then Jerry spoke again. "Darnedest thing is that for forty years these postcards go unclaimed, and now you're the second folks to come here asking about them in two days."

Gabe and I froze. I turned.

"Someone else asked about them?"

"Yup. Big feller. I remember his feet in particular."

"Did you give him a postcard?" Gabe asked.

"Nope. He didn't seem as interested in them as you. Just wanted the address."

Gabe and I ran out the door yelling for Sam.

There was no mistaking it—the historian *was* on the same quest we were.

And he was ahead of us.

The race was on.

CHAPTER 19

We

Sam was nowhere to be found.

After a minute, we stopped calling for her and leaned against the car to wait. I could feel the heat of the metal through my sweater.

The sun was blazing in the cloudless sky.

"I'm starting to sweat," I said. "Where's your stupid sister?"

"Hey!" Gabe said. "That's not nice."

"Whatever. We've got to get moving."

"Maybe you could take off your sweater?"

"I'd rather die." I wiped beads of sweat off my forehead.

Gabe started to walk toward the post office. "Maybe we should go back inside?" he suggested. "It's cooler."

"No!" I said, shuffling and looking up and down the street. "We want to be ready to bolt the *second* your sister finally gets back."

"It'll be, like, a three-second difference," Gabe said.

"Three more seconds the historian will gain on us."

Gabe stared at me like I was loco, but he rejoined me by the car.

"Have you got heatstroke?" he asked.

"I've got historian stroke," I said. "My quest is turning into a joke." I slapped my hand against the side of the car. But instead of a satisfactory clunk, the metal made a kind of sickly rattle.

"Careful," Gabe said with a chuckle. "We don't want to break Rusty."

"Gabe, I am not in the mood for jokes."

He leaned back against the car and hung his head. "Okay, sure."

We didn't say anything else for what seemed like hours.

"Do you think your sister abandoned us? This is ridiculous."

"Why do you keep calling Sam 'your sister'?" Gabe asked.

"Fine. Sam. Whatever." Images of the historian racing farther and farther ahead filled my brain. The sun got hotter and I did too.

"I wonder who the historian could be?" Gabe finally said, watching a tumbleweed slowly make its way down the middle of the road. "It's pretty amazing that someone else is figuring out Taylor's clues."

Wait. Did Gabe seem excited?

He was still talking. "I wonder if he figured out the church address in Arcadia? Oh! And he definitely got the post-card stuff. You'd have to be totally clueless to miss that one. But did he see Lysander's grave after we cleared the vines from it? And if he's on the same track, it means we were right about the clues so far!"

I clenched and unclenched my fists. "We. We. WE. Who's 'we,' Gabe? You and the tall guy? You seem so happy, maybe you want *him* to find it first?"

His mouth snapped shut. He narrowed his eyes. "Zed, you're being a pain."

"*I'm* being a pain?" I began to yell. "*You're* being a jerk! If you hadn't posted that stuff about place names on the site, the historian wouldn't even be on this trip! Now he's ahead of me!"

I slapped the car again.

"Ahead of 'me'?" Gabe said.

"Yes! He was a couple of hours ahead in Arcadia. And now he's two days ahead." I stabbed a finger in the air. "And it's all. Your. Fault."

Gabe pushed himself away from the car. He took a deep breath. "I think you need to cool down, Zed," he said. "Let's go back inside the post office."

"Do not tell me what to do."

Gabe's face grew red. "Zed—" He started to say something, then stopped. When he opened his mouth again, it was like a volcano erupting. "If I hadn't made that post, YOU wouldn't have any idea either!" He began waving his arms. "Did you know what Rosaceae meant? No. What a *memento mori* was? No! No, Zed. *I* did. *Me.*"

I stood there, speechless.

"Nothing to say? For once?"

Gabe's words hit me like a punch in the gut. Had I actually said this was "my" trip?

I ran the conversation back in my head.

I *had* said it. *I* was being the jerk.

I had never seen Gabe like this. It made me sad and ashamed. It was my fault.

My shoulders sagged.

"Gabe—" I started.

"What? You want to criticize my love of opera? Or flowers? Like all the other jerks at school or my stupid dad—" He stopped suddenly; his arms fell. He looked like a balloon that had just been popped, and he turned away from me. "Zed, you love this book, but I do too. This isn't *your* trip. It's *our* trip. Ours. Or I don't want to be on it anymore."

"Gabe, I . . ." I wasn't sure what I could say. But I needed to say something. "I'm so sorry. I don't want to criticize you for anything."

"Sure." He shrugged.

"Hey, what's with the racket?" asked Sam as she walked up holding a brown paper bag. "What's going on?"

"Nothing," Gabe said. "Let's go." He reached over to open his door.

Sam looked at me and cocked her head. "Um, Zed?"

"Can you give us a minute?" I asked.

"Sure," Sam said. She got in the driver's seat and turned on the car. The engine rumbled as the A/C kicked in.

I walked over to Gabe, who was just standing there with his hand on the door handle.

"Gabe, you are one million percent right. This is *our* trip." I sighed. "Back in Mantua, I said stuff does bug me. This is one of those times."

"Zed—" he began.

I held up my hand. "No. I'm not making an excuse. It's just an explanation. I was acting like that hot-headed soldier Marion and Cassandra meet. The one who started the Battle of Thistlethorn."

"Which we have no idea who wins," Gabe said.

"Yeah. Cassandra keeps trying to convince him to calm down. But he just refuses to listen. And then he fires that spectral-haze bomb and it's too late."

166

Gabe gave a weak smile. "Stupid guy."

"I'm that stupid guy right now. But you're Cassandra, and I'm going to listen."

"Cassandra is pretty awesome."

"You are too, Gabe." I practically leapt over and hugged him. "I know you want to find this book too. Let's go find it together, deal?"

He smiled. "Deal," he said.

We shook hands.

Sam rolled down her window. "Ahem. Can we get back on the road now?"

"Sure," Gabe said.

He opened the door, and we got in the back seat.

My stomach growled, loudly.

"That sounds like a hungry Zed," Sam said. "Lucky for you, I found some sandwiches at a place down the street. Not bad, actually." She tossed the paper bag to me.

I eagerly pulled out two amazing-smelling sandwiches in folded wax paper.

"Yours is the greasy one."

I unwrapped the paper.

"Brie cheese and pear!" I jumped forward and hugged Sam's shoulders.

"And a kale Caesar wrap!" Gabe seemed more excited than me. "Thanks, Sis!"

"You're welcome. So, Scooby-Doo and Scooby-Don't, everything cool between you?"

We already had half the sandwiches stuffed in our mouths, so we just nodded our heads.

"Good." She put Rusty in gear and began driving away. "You two eat up while we burn some rubber. Then we can look for an ice cream shop for dessert."

Gabe and I exchanged a look. Our argument had added even more time to the historian's lead.

Stopping for ice cream was now a luxury.

"No time," Gabe said.

I smiled. "Yeah. WE need to keep moving."

"Moving where exactly?" Sam asked.

Gabe munched quietly on his kale wrap while I swallowed some pear and Brie. I saw he was going to be no help on this one. I cleared my throat.

"Yeah, about that . . ." I started.

I didn't know how to tell Sam that we weren't sure.

CHAPTER 20

Dolly Carton

In fact, we did end up stopping for ice cream.

Well, actually, we stopped for gas, but it seemed like every dust-covered gas station on the highway also served desserts.

Ice cream sandwiches were on the menu at the Gas-n-Stuff (which I immediately dubbed the Gassy Stuff). These sandwiches were a pale imitation of actual ice cream, but they had to do in a pinch. I swallowed my pride, and then three of the sandwiches.

They also tasted better because they were Gabe's treat. I'd accurately predicted that the sweet old lady with the tiny eyeglasses at the checkout counter would call me a boy.

Gabe pulled his notebook out of—you guessed it—a pocket of his pants and updated the tally.

"Boy 6, girl 5," he announced. Then the notebook disappeared.

"Where do you hide those?" I asked, impressed.

"Wouldn't you like to know?" Gabe smiled mischievously.

"Yes. That's why I asked. I assume you have some hidden compartments in your shoes, because those pockets should be bulging with all the stuff you jam in there."

Gabe just nibbled on his vanilla ice cream sandwich and looked out the window.

I continued my observations. "It's because they're boys' pants. Girls' pants have smaller pockets. How do I know this, you ask?"

"I did?"

I ignored the interruption. "You may have noticed that I do not, as a rule, wear pants—and certainly not jeans. Sometimes chinos or corduroys, but only in a pinch—I prefer either my current choice of sweatpants, featuring what is known as a Memphis pattern—"

Sam snorted from the front seat. "Very stylish, Zed."

Gabe looked at my sweats, which I had just changed into, featuring neon-blue squiggles and yellow triangles with green semicircles.

"That's a Memphis pattern?" he asked.

Sam laughed. "It looks like a math textbook threw up on your legs."

This elicited a snort from Gabe.

"Or if I am feeling jaunty," I continued, "I often choose patterned leggings with pictures of taco shells or cats. My core idea about clothes is that you can never be *too* flamboyant."

"You sure about that?" Sam said.

"I simply like visual excitement in my clothes. It's like the writer and flamboyant icon Oscar Wilde once said: 'One should either be a work of art, or wear a work of art.' And I happen to achieve both."

Gabe slow-clapped, and I gave a little bow.

"Now, to answer your question about pants."

"Ah, yes," Gabe said, "that imaginary question I didn't ask."

"I was once forced to buy actual blue jeans." I made a quick gagging noise. "This was for a school trip to a factory or something. No sandals allowed."

I held up my sandaled feet.

"No baggy clothing."

I pointed to my sweatpants and amazing sweater.

"And students needed to wear denim for 'safety.' I have never felt so attacked!" I shook my head in

disgust. "But my parents took me to the store, and I looked in every aisle for something that wasn't horrible. I did not succeed."

"You didn't go on the field trip?" Gabe asked.

"I said I didn't find any jeans that weren't horrible—but I did find a pair. So I wore them once and then handed them down to one of my siblings."

Sam looked at me strangely in the mirror. "They actually made you buy new clothes to go on a field trip?"

"Well, not exactly," I said. "The other option was to cover your normal clothes with a bright orange safety smock. I mean, not this kid!"

Sam rolled her eyes for like the thousandth time.

"You're going to need a new prescription if you keep that up," I said. "And shouldn't you be looking at the road?"

She growled but turned her attention back to the highway.

We were passing some town. Green trees were giving way to billboards and motels. Those soon gave way to more trees and bushes. And so on.

It had been like this for hours, and we expected it to be much the same for hours to come.

This was the longest stretch of driving yet.

And as I had started to admit to Sam, we weren't exactly sure where we were heading. We had some coordinates that pointed southwest, which was where

Sam was heading anyway, but the next stop on the road trip was unclear.

The postcards had said "Come dine with me." But where?

The clues in the fifth stanza of the poem and the corresponding chapter fragment weren't as obvious to us as the other three had been. It wasn't just the coordinates that had pointed us in the right direction. The fragment was all about a dinner between Lysander and Yves. Both it and the poem referenced a rare type of plant that blooms only at night. And Gabe knew that this plant grew only in the southwestern US. But what were we looking for?

A restaurant at a botanical garden?

A greenhouse that served french fries?

Doubts nagged at us.

Were we missing something?

I desperately wanted to check the fan site to see if there were any more comments that might help us solve this riddle.

"How about *Eugene Onegin*?" It was Gabe's voice.

"Who?" I asked. "I don't remember him from the book."

Gabe looked at me strangely. "I think you were having a Zed moment. Sam and I are wondering which opera to sing along to."

I slumped in my seat. "Opera. The denim blue jeans of music."

"*Onegin* it is," Sam said.

They began singing some high-pitched opera thing in what I think was Klingon. I stared out the window and waited for it to be over. But—and I hate to admit this—after a little while, I quite liked it. The music was totally dramatic, and Gabe filled me in on the story.

"It's this tragic romance about a guy named Onegin who moves to a new place and meets a woman named Tatiana. She falls in love with him, but he rejects her."

This really emotional song came on next, with this woman singing about how hard it is to find the words to tell someone how much you love them.

I even choked up a bit. "It helps to know what's going on," I said.

Gabe was singing along with the woman, so he just nodded at me.

All of a sudden, Rusty made a high-pitched whining noise.

"Aww, Rusty is trying to sing along too!" I said.

But Sam immediately switched off the music and started cranking the steering wheel.

Rusty continued whining. It sounded worse now, like a huge bunch of nails and marbles being shaken in a jar during a thunderstorm.

We began to slow down, right in the middle of the highway. A truck zoomed past us on the right. There was an exit just ahead.

"Hit the gas," I said, starting to panic.

"Get off the highway!" Gabe said, pointing at the exit.

"Quiet!" Sam said. She hit the hazard lights, opened her window and began frantically waving her hand in the air.

I looked out the rear window. There were only a few trucks and cars, but they were moving fast, and we weren't.

"What's happening?" I said.

"I'm trying to get us out of here!" Sam yelled.

The car drivers saw her waving and slowed to let us get in the right lane.

Rusty rolled and rolled but continued to slow. We were almost at the exit.

I looked out the back window. A truck was heading toward the same exit we were.

"MOVE!" I yelled.

The truck began blaring its horn. The exit had only one lane—and we were now in it.

Gabe and I screamed, "I don't want to die!"

Sam turned the wheel sharply, and we rolled off the side of the road.

The truck honked loudly and sped past us, zooming up the exit ramp.

"Jerk!" yelled Sam, still struggling with the wheel.

Rusty began sliding down into the ditch. Sam slammed on the brakes, but we continued to go down the muddy bank.

Gabe started screaming, so I screamed too.

Gabe's head smacked the top of the car, and my teeth clacked in my mouth.

Then suddenly, we stopped.

All three of us jolted forward. My head almost collided with the seat in front of me, but I was pulled up short by my seat belt.

I kept screaming, "I DON'T WANT TO DIE! I'M TOO ADORABLE!" until my voice was suddenly much louder than any other noise. I realized that Sam and Gabe had both stopped and were looking at me.

"Don't kid yourself, Watson," said Sam, and for a second, I was quiet.

But then for some reason, what she said seemed so funny to me, and I started laughing. Soon we were all laughing, even Sam.

Then, like the car, we slowed and stopped.

Sam gave a tired sigh. "I'm going to see what's up with the car. Don't go anywhere."

I opened my mouth to make a joke, like, "Where would I go without a car? The moon?" But Gabe was starting to know me too well and shot me a warning look, so I closed my mouth and said nothing.

Sam got out and walked to the front of the car. We watched her through the windshield as she strained to open the hood.

A cloud of thick black smoke poured out and obscured Sam almost completely. Gabe gasped and unbuckled himself, then he was out the door in a flash. I could hear Sam's raised voice, and then I could see them arguing as the smoke cleared. I got out too because I didn't want to be left out of the action.

"Zed! What did I JUST say?!" Sam waved her arms angrily at me.

"I just wanted to make sure you guys were okay! Rusty tried to kill us!" I protested.

She opened her mouth to make some retort, but then looked confused. "Wait. Who's Rusty?"

"You're looking at him, Sam," I said, pointing to the mess in front of us.

Sam folded her arms. "Her *name* is Dolly Carton."

I stared at the Impreza in shock. "At least Dolly Parton works nine to five," I said. "Dolly Carton doesn't seem to be working at all."

Sam shook her head and turned her attention back to the engine. She closed her eyes, and for a second, I was scared she was going to cry.

"Are you okay?"

"Yes!" she snapped. "I'm just trying to think." She tinkered with some cables and lines but eventually slammed the hood and gave the bumper a kick.

"So . . . what do we do now?" Gabe asked.

"Yeah, the historian is gaining more ground the longer we stand here!"

Sam turned around. "Your little quest is the least of our problems right now. Got it?"

"Little? LITTLE?"

She pointed a finger at me. "Don't. Just don't." She gave a frustrated scream and kicked the bumper again.

Someone needed to take charge, and that someone was going to be me.

I cleaned off my glasses with a tissue and activated what my dad calls my Zed-O-Vision.

CHAPTER 21

Zed-O-Vision

Zed-O-Vision is a gift that seems to come when needed most. At least that's what my dad says. I'm amazing at finding emergency public washrooms, hotdog vendors, ATMs and, right now, a gas station.

I locked my eyes on a speck up ahead. It had a roughly rectangular shape, and even with the heat rising off the asphalt, I could tell the flat top was the overhang of a gas station.

I pointed at it. "Do you think they would know where we could get someone to fix Rusty?"

Sam squinted at where I was pointing. "How did you even see that?"

"Zed-O-Vision."

"Vision?" Gabe said. "I've tried your glasses on, and you have literally the strongest prescription of anyone I know."

I shrugged. "What can I say? Zed-O-Vision is a gift."

Gabe peered at the speck. "GPS has nothing on those peepers."

"Okay, I'm cutting this little Zed-preciation session short," Sam said. "Can I trust you guys to be safe and go to the gas station to see if they know someone or have someone who can help us fix Dolly?"

"Rusty," I said.

"You mean Dolly? Your one and only chance of getting anywhere close to the dopey book you want?"

"Yeah, Dolly," I said. "That's what I meant."

"Good. Now as soon as you get to the station, call my cell and let me know what's up. I'll stay with the car and our gear. And maybe I can get enough juice to at least get us out of the ditch."

"Aye, aye," Gabe and I said with mock salutes.

Then we started walking.

The ditch had seemed like the Grand Canyon when we were sliding into it, but really it was just a little slope with some weeds and water at the bottom. We skirted the top until the shoulder got wider and then we started walking on that. We kept the steel barrier between us and the road.

I looked back and watched Sam flex her muscles and start pushing Rusty—or I guess I should say Dolly—little by little back to the shoulder of the road.

"Sam, you are a force," I whispered.

"Yes, she is," Gabe said.

We walked for a little bit in silence. The sun beat down.

"Whew. It's hot," I said.

"No kidding. And it's not a dry heat either."

"It's like someone wrapped a damp blanket around us."

"A damp blanket that's been microwaved," Gabe added.

"Well done," I said.

"Not yet," he replied with a smile. "I think I'm only medium rare. But give it a few more minutes."

"Gabe, you are opening up like a rose under my guidance. I couldn't be prouder."

"And I've even got you listening to opera. I couldn't be prouder."

We reached a crossroads.

"Where's the gas station?" Gabe asked.

"Well, it should be right around here." I scanned the horizon. I looked back and could still see Sam and the car in the distance.

I groaned. "What if the gas station was just a mirage? What if I got so hot and scared that I hallucin-ated an oasis, like people do in the Sahara Desert?"

"You saw it before we started walking in this heat," Gabe said. "It's real. And I saw it too. It must be close."

I activated the Zed-O-Vision again and looked forward. "It's still up ahead! But even with my awe-some powers, I can't believe I saw that far!"

Gabe smiled. "Ah. Science again."

"Science?"

"It's because of the heat."

"So I *was* imagining it?"

"No. It's an effect that happens in hot air. The light gets bent and you can see faraway things, but they seem way closer."

"Whoa," I said.

"Science is cool."

"Let's hope the gas station is too."

It took another ten minutes, but we finally arrived. There were no cars at the pumps. The white paint was peeling off the cinderblock. The windows were so covered in posters for pop and snacks that it was hard to tell if there were lights on inside.

"Maybe it's haunted!" I said, a thrill running down my spine. I pushed open the door and walked in.

The inside was packed tighter than our trunk. Shelves from floor to ceiling were jammed with all kinds of weird stuff: touristy knickknacks, bobbleheads of old presidents, what looked like handmade quilts, signs with biblical sayings and even a kitchen sink.

There was no one in sight.

"HELLO?" I bellowed.

Gabe shuffled around nervously.

A man about Uncle Amir's age poked his head around a shelf that was overflowing with various kinds of canned foods. He was wearing a flannel shirt with a puffy vest that looked like it was made from an old sleeping bag.

"Pattern mixing," I said. "I respect that."

He had a name tag that said "Leslie."

"Can I help you? Need to pay for gas?" he asked.

"Actually," I said, "we are in need of—" Then I stopped.

Leslie had moved a bit, revealing a desk with an ancient-looking computer and a

sign that read, "Internet: $2 per half hour. No video or audio. Thanks."

"Leslie, can I use the computer?" I asked.

"I don't know. Can ya?"

"What the heck?" Gabe said. "Zed . . ."

But Leslie was already moving aside to let me pass. "Sure you *may*. It's a trust system. Just drop the money in the box there."

I shot past him.

"Zed!" Gabe said.

"The quest must go on," I called back over my shoulder. I woke up the computer, which slowly hummed to life.

Gabe took over the conversation with Leslie.

"Actually, we were wondering if you know someone who could fix our car. We're just stopped on the side of the highway."

"You sure about that, son? You two don't look old enough to drive." He chuckled.

I chuckled too. I kind of dig that old-guy humor, but Gabe earnestly replied, "Oh, don't worry. I'm not driving."

"Yeah, figured that, bucko."

"My sister is. She's back with the car."

They continued to chat, but I stopped listening. Then I felt a tap on my shoulder.

"Hey, kid, you have to pay *before* you can use the computer. Minimum is two bucks."

I turned and looked into the face of a frowning woman wearing dirty overalls and what was once a white T-shirt. She had muscles that could give Sam's a run for their money. She was pointing at the cash box and raising an eyebrow at me.

I gulped.

"Oops?" I'd been in such a hurry to check the site, I had forgotten to pay. Sheepishly, I pulled out my smiley-face wallet and produced two one-dollar bills. I folded them so they fit into the slot and tapped them gently until they disappeared.

The woman smiled at me.

"Thanks," she said. Then she laughed. "I think that's the first two bucks we've made in about five years."

I held out my hand. "Hello, I'm Zed, and my pronouns are they/them/theirs."

"Jo. She/her/hers." She took off her hat, a grease-covered conductor-type one, and bowed slightly. Then she put the hat back on, backward. She looked pretty cool.

"Tell me, Jo, am I mistaken or does that getup"—and here I waved my arm toward her overalls and work boots—"mean that you are someone who can fix a car?"

Jo smirked. "You're right, Zed. I can." She fished in her back pocket for a rag and showed it to me. "Auto grease. A good mechanic gets it on her clothes, not on her hands."

At that moment, Gabe came over. "Zed, stop wasting time! Leslie says his cousin is a mechanic and can—"

"Might her name be Jo?" I asked.

Gabe's mouth dropped open. "What are you, psychic?"

"Just chatty," Jo said. She stuck out her hand. "I'm Jo."

Gabe shook it. "And you can fix cars?"

"Cars that can be fixed. I'm no miracle worker."

"In that case, we may be out of luck," I joked.

Jo gave me a wink. "Well, let's see about that. Where's the car?"

"Back near the highway," Gabe said.

"Unless Sam's been able to push it up the hill." I laughed. "Even with all the rocks in the trunk."

Jo got a weird look on her face. "Sam? Rocks?"

"Yeah," I said. "She's built like a rock too. Studies geology. Gabe's sister."

Jo's face lit up. "You have got to be kidding me! Not Sam Linden?!"

"Um, you know my sister?" Gabe asked.

"Sort of. We're in the same program at school. Done some geocaching stuff together. We call her Samson because she's so strong." Jo flexed her own muscles. "And she has amazing hair."

"Whoa," I said. "This is fate! Taylor's book is magic!"

Gabe nodded. "It all feels meant to be," he added. He didn't mention the historian, but we were both probably thinking about him too. I tried to put him out of my mind and focus on getting Jo to the car.

We asked Leslie if there was a phone so we could call Sam with the good news. He pointed at some ancient blue plastic thing on the wall.

I dialed Sam's cell.

She didn't even wait for me to say anything. Her voice boomed from the earpiece. "Zed? What took so long? Any luck? Or should I grab my rocks and start thumbing for rides—*alone*?"

I looked at Jo.

"Yup, that's her," she said with a laugh. "This is so wild."

I leaned into the mouthpiece. "I dunno, *Samson*. Would a buff mechanic named Jo fit the bill?"

Sam took a second to respond. "A buff mechanic named Jo would be . . . perfect."

CHAPTER 22

Historian Hijinks

"Not coming for the ride?" Jo asked, standing by the open back door. A muddy brown tow truck was parked on the gravel lot a few feet away.

"Nice try," I said, staying seated in front of the computer. "Force me to pay my two bucks, then yank me away."

"Yup. That's the kind of sketchy business model that has me and Les rolling in dough." She gestured to the stacks of knickknacks and dust-covered boxes.

Leslie frowned and wiped away a fake tear. "You may recollect, Jo, that you are a mere summer employee. Whereas I am the sole proprietor and owner of this treasure trove."

"Treasure?" Jo said with a smirk. "You mean junk."

Leslie held up his palms. "Maybe there's a lamp hidden in the stacks with a wish-granting genie inside." He looked at me and winked. "Just got to say the magic words, and unknown riches await."

I laughed.

"Uh-huh," Jo said. "Well, I'll go make some real money and see if we can get this Dolly Carton of theirs back on the road. Gabe, are you coming?"

Gabe looked torn. I could tell he wanted to stay, but he also wanted to see what a reunion between Samson and Jo might look like. I admit I was also debating. But I really wanted to check the fan site.

"Psst. You go spy on the rock-heads," I said to Gabe, "and I'll report back on anything I find on the site. You'll all be back here in a few minutes anyway."

"Okay, cool," he said. "See you in a few."

He walked toward the tow truck.

"And, Gabe," I called, "take pictures."

He smiled and gave a thumbs-up. The door closed behind him with a creak.

Leslie shuffled back to the front of the store. "Well, Zed, you have fun looking at the Twittlers and Faceboats and such. I guess I'll keep searching for that lamp."

I hit a random key on the keyboard and the computer blipped back to life.

I typed in the address for the *Monster's Castle* fan site, then navigated slowly through the pages until I found Gabe's original post: "Has anyone ever considered the possibility that the weird stuff and the flowers in the poem and the fragments are actually clues about place names?"

There were twenty new comments. And five new members!

Wow. The legion was growing, and they were also chatting.

"Inspired by our noble quest, no doubt," I said to the screen.

"What was that?" Leslie called from somewhere among the shelves.

"Sorry. Just talking to myself."

"Okay. And I'm just talking to my shelf." He chuckled and started moving more of his treasure around.

I scrolled past the comments I'd already read, including the one from @Hi_Its_Another: "How are you sure this is the right path?"

The comment had made me anxious just a couple of days before. But we were finding the clues and heading in the right direction. I planned to add our latest discoveries and location to the site at the end of the thread.

The new comments were mostly more notes of encouragement.

Let Taylor's monsters LIVE!!!
The world is ready and waiting.

But then there were two that made me pause.

One was from another new member, @Times_Lisa: "Been following your quest. Fascinating. Can we talk?"

Weren't we talking on the fan site? Did @Times_ Lisa have some info that could help?

Or was it the opposite?

My mom was always warning me about the dangers of being online. And I'd been posting where we were and where we were going.

And now someone was "following" us. There was nothing in Gabe's or my profile that suggested we were kids. But my danger-meter was now turned on.

Maybe I'd hold off posting any more locations until we were back home. With the book!

I simply typed back, "Always willing to talk. About what? And who are you? Specifics."

A couple more messages said, "GO FOR IT!!!"

And then I read the final comment and froze.

@Hi_Its_Another was back.

Been working out the clues @TheFabulousZW has been posting.

    Nice work, ZW.

    But I've been sketching out a map, and I think you're wrong.

Wrong?

Message me to hear more, but I'm almost one hundred percent positive *The Monster's Castle* is hidden in South Carolina.

Any Taylor fans in the area who would like to meet up and find it, let me know.

ZW, you're welcome too.

I should have the book in my hands by the end of the week.

The message had been posted two days before.

South Carolina?

That was in the exact opposite direction. It would take days to turn around and get there.

Had we messed up the clues?

The coordinates?

Then a horrible thought popped into my head.

Had Sam *lied* to us?

She needed to be in Arizona in a few days to start school. What if she knew the coordinates we'd found were for a completely different direction? We were trusting her to tell us where the coordinates pointed. But maybe she'd made sure we still headed to where *she* needed to go?

No. I shook my head. Sam couldn't be working against us. Could she?

Or had we all got the numbers mixed up?

We were just two dumb kids and one dumb sorta-adult. What did we know? This @Hi_Its_Another person had time and resources we didn't have on the road. And they were *certain* they'd figured it out.

I don't know how long I sat there staring at the

screen, thinking horrible thoughts. I do know that I almost jumped out of my skin when Leslie tapped me on the shoulder. The screen had gone dark.

"Goodness, didn't mean to startle ya! Just making some tea. Want some?"

I couldn't even speak. I opened my mouth, but my throat was so tight no sound came out, so I just shook my head.

"Okay," Leslie said. "No tea for thee, Zee."

"I'll take some tea!" Gabe said.

Gabe? When did he get back?

How long had I been Zed-ding out?

And if Gabe was back, that meant—

Sam ruffled my hair.

"Hey, Zed. Find anything nerdy? Well, nerdier than usual."

I swung around and found my voice. "I've just been on the fan site." I narrowed my eyes at Sam.

"Uh-huh," she said.

"Someone named @Hi_Its_Another says the book is in *South Carolina*! We're totally one hundred percent the stupidest people in the world," I said. "Unless one of us isn't stupid . . . but evil."

Sam leaned away from me. "I know who I'd vote for," she said.

I started to shake. "You've never really cared about this book or this quest, have you?"

"Zed, what is this about?"

Gabe walked over, blowing on his tea. "Everything okay?"

"No! No!" I said. "How do we know your sister isn't lying about the GPS coordinates?"

Sam scrunched up her face.

"SEE!" I said. "The look of guilt! She *needs* us to go to Arizona."

Sam said nothing.

Gabe looked at his sister but shook his head. "No way," he said, but I was sure I detected a slight quiver in his voice.

Sam was now glaring at me.

"Move," she said. "Now."

"I'm not going anywhere with you."

"I want to show you something, goofball. So move!"

Her neck muscles were twitching. I think I heard them crunch.

Maybe direct confrontation hadn't been my wisest choice.

I slid my chair sideways. Actually, Sam slid my chair sideways with just one finger, and I kind of shuffled my feet.

She leaned down and started typing on the computer. Then she stood back up and pointed at the screen.

Gabe and I leaned in.

"I typed the coordinates we have into Google Maps," she said.

A red dot hovered over the southwest corner of New Mexico. The direction we were heading.

"Oh," I said.

"Yeah," Sam said. "We could even go straight there now, without the final longitudinal coordinates. It would take a lot of digging, but we might find this dopey book—in a decade."

"Oh," I said again.

"And you're being such a total pain in my butt right now, I can think of another use for digging holes."

"She means as a grave," Gabe whispered to me.

"I got it," I said. My face was burning.

"You have a great imagination, kid," Sam said. "Just rein it in a little bit, okay?"

"Okay," I said. "But why would @Hi_Its_Another tell me to meet them in South Carolina?"

"They're either stupid," Sam said, "or evil."

Just then, Jo walked in covered in grease.

"Well, I've got good news and bad news. Which do you want to hear first?"

CHAPTER 23

Bad News, Okay Grub

Before we could answer, Jo noticed the computer screen. "Your half hour ended a while back, Zed. You owe another two bucks."

I slid two more dollar bills into the slot. I was starting to run low on the cash my mom and dad had given me.

"Thanks," Jo said. "I'll skip to the good news. Dolly Carton will ride again!"

We gave out a huge cheer.

"But?" Sam said. "The bad news?"

"But I need to get a part from another garage owned by a friend of mine. I've called and they'll have it here . . . tomorrow."

We gave out a huge groan.

"That's it," I said. "Quest over. Either the book is in South Carolina—"

"It's *not*," Sam said.

"Or the historian is racing toward it and will get there first."

I wiped my face on my sleeve (another pro of big sweaters) and ran my fingers under my eyes to catch any spare tears. Even Rusty felt like my fault—the car never would have busted if I hadn't been pushing us to go faster and harder. Basically everything was ruined.

Gabe put a hand on my shoulder. "Zed, we're doing all we can. Maybe the historian is reading the site too. Maybe *he's* heading to South Carolina!"

The thought cheered me up a bit. Then my stomach grumbled.

"Hey, Leslie," I said. "You don't have any gourmet food hidden in those boxes, do you?"

"As a matter of fact . . ."

My spirits started to rise.

"No."

"Oh."

"But I do have a nice stew in the freezer. I'll see if it's still any good."

. . . .

We sat around a picnic table in the backyard. Jo had pinned a stained gingham cloth over the table.

"It's like Dorothy's dress!" I said.

The stew was not bad at all. Chunks of beef. Big bits of veggies for Gabe. And there were other strange things that I needed Leslie to explain.

"Well, I call it the Oklahoma stew," he said. "A

while back, the state named an official meal with all these different parts. Fried okra."

"That's the long green bit," Gabe said, slurping one into his mouth.

Leslie nodded. "And then I kind of throw in other stuff. Some squash. Sausage and gravy with grits. Bits of leftover pork. Chicken-fried steak and black-eyed peas."

Jo scooped some into a bowl and handed it to me with a piece of corn bread. "Supposed to reflect all the cuisines from the people who live, or lived, here."

"Well, it's all okay by me!" I said, grabbing a spoonful.

Jo actually spat out the corn bread she was chewing. "That's hilarious!" she said.

I was confused. "What did I say?"

"You said it was all okay."

"And? Sorry, was that an insult? I haven't even tasted it yet."

"It's not that," Sam said. "That's where we are. Okay, Oklahoma!"

"Okay, Oklahoma," I repeated. "Seems like another good omen."

"You can hope," she said, and tucked back into her stew.

After dinner, we lit a huge bonfire. Leslie turned in early.

"You kids have fun. I'll see you in the morning."

"Not if I see you first," I said.

"I like you, kid," he said. "You're funny." He winked again and left, carrying the leftovers in a huge bin. He refused to let any of us help clean up.

I was thinking about Leslie, the feast, the quest and all sorts of things a bit later. We'd been so close.

Had Gabe and I failed? Would we ever find the book? I was shaken out of this latest Zed moment by a huge laugh.

Sam had her head tossed back, and Jo was smirking.

"That *is* funny," Gabe said, laughing too.

"What's funny?" I asked.

Sam waved a hand. "You had to be there."

"I *was* there! I was just distracted."

Jo leaned forward, hands on her knees. "I was just saying that I've got some serious *dirt* on this girl!" She shot a thumb toward Sam.

Sam and Gabe laughed again.

"I don't get it."

"DIRT!" Jo prompted. "Get it? Because we're geologists?"

It was like a Leslie pun! I laughed. "Funny. In fact, that joke *rocked*."

"Yeah. We really *dig* your jokes," Gabe said.

"*Pyrite* you are!" Sam added.

"Ha! *Shale* I give you another? *Ore* would you prefer something else?"

Which, of course, set off another round.

The pun battle eventually died down, and so did the fire.

We set up our tents in the twilight, ignoring the hovering bugs, then watched the embers glowing underneath the stars. I had grabbed the marshmallows from the car, and Gabe and I happily made s'mores.

"How can you two eat so close to bedtime?" Sam asked.

I pointed at my head. "Our amazing brains need energy."

"They need something," she agreed. Then she gave Jo a hug. "Thanks for saving our butts today."

"I haven't saved anyone's butts until tomorrow. And it's nice to have some people around. Been a slow summer."

It hit me that we'd been about the only customers to visit the station all day. Leslie had filled up a few gas tanks, but not a lot.

"Where is everybody?" I asked.

"Used to be a very busy stop," Jo said. "But then a lot of the factories and stuff closed. Not just here but all around. Now people don't take the highway unless they're heading somewhere else, fast."

"Like we were," Gabe said.

"But a lucky breakdown for all of us, I guess," Sam said. "In a way."

"Well, we did make four bucks off the computer," Jo said. "So that's something."

"Does Leslie ever sell any of that stuff?" I asked.

Jo sighed. "He used to. It's actually all stuff he's made himself. Carved plaques. Weirdest thing he does is collect roadkill and stuff it."

"Seriously? Like taxidermy?" Gabe asked.

"Yup. He says it's a shame the way people leave

those poor creatures out there. So he wants to give them some dignity. He'll show you if you ask him."

I was definitely asking, just as soon as Leslie was awake!

"So, Jo, why are you here?" I asked.

"I work as a mechanic during the summer to pay off my student loans. This is my base, but I also do work at other garages along the highway. Wherever I'm needed, really. I grew up with my mom doing it, so it was just a natural progression, I guess."

Sam cut in. "Plus, you know, you're really good at it. Remember the time you fixed the Jeep when it broke down on the Guatemala trip?"

Jo laughed. "You bring that up like it was so amazing, but it basically just needed an oil change. It wasn't a big deal!"

I may have been hovering on the border of despair all day, but I know a potential IRL romance when I see one.

And it perked me up.

Sam kept brushing hair from her eyes. Jo laughed at almost everything Sam said.

I'd spent a lot of time with Sam over the previous few days, and take it from me, she is NOT that funny.

My head volleyed between the two.

I looked over and noticed Gabe doing the same thing.

We caught each other's eye and smiled.

Chapter 24

Aloysius

The part arrived first thing in the morning.

Jo and Sam got to work doing life-saving surgery on Rusty . . . um, Dolly . . . well, the car.

Laughter and also a few howls of pain came from the garage.

I slipped another two bucks into the computer bin, but no one had updated the fan site in the last few hours. I'd try to check in again later. It sounded like we'd still be stuck here for a while.

Finally, Leslie appeared.

I practically jumped on him as he flipped the sign on the front door from Closed to Open.

"LESLIE!"

He did jump. "Whoa! That's a loud pre-coffee greeting, young Zed. Just give me a second."

"But I want to see your gallery!"

His eyes twinkled. "Jo told you about that? I'd be glad to—after coffee."

I stood around impatiently as his ancient coffee

maker dripped and dripped liquid as thick as molasses into his mug.

The mug had "Don't talk to me until I've eaten this mug" written across it. I suspected that he'd made it himself.

Gabe came in through the back door, yawning and stretching.

"Shhhh," I said, pointing at Leslie. "He's not alive yet."

Gabe nodded and grabbed a granola bar from a nearby shelf. He sat on the floor, munching away.

Finally, after a second cup of coffee and one paying customer, Leslie gave a satisfied "Ahhhhh." "Strong enough to raise the dead," he said.

"See, Gabe? Told you."

"C'mon, let's go visit my critters."

We followed him between the stacks toward a locked wooden door. Honestly, it was like a labyrinth in this place.

A sign on the door said Leslie's Magnificent Menagerie. He opened it, revealing the coolest room I had ever seen!

Inside were skunks playing miniature violins. A fox stood in front of an easel, painting a version of the *Mona Lisa*. Two cats danced under a flying squirrel holding the moon.

And staring at me from a pedestal along the back wall, with almost a smile, was a long-eared rabbit with deer antlers.

"Is that a real jackalope?" I said in an awed hush.

"Well, as real as they can be. You know about them?" Leslie asked with a smile.

"They are the coolest fake animals EVER! Practically monsters! Taylor even throws a reference into one of the chapters. Yves the werewolf has one as a pet."

"Aloysius," Gabe said. "Part hare, part deer."

Just mentioning Yves and Aloysius made me anxious. I hoped Jo was as good a mechanic as she was a punster because we needed to be back on the road.

I cocked an ear and heard the ding of metal and then Sam swearing.

Gabe heard it too. "Sounds like progress?" he said.

"I think we're still gonna be here for a bit," I said, and I walked straight up to the jackalope. "Hello, little feller."

I imagined it, I know, but he twitched his nose in return.

Gabe walked up beside me. "He looks so alive! Nice work, Leslie."

"You like him?" Leslie said.

"I *love* him!" I said, stroking the soft downy fur.

"Well, he is for sale, like all my animals. I want him to find a good home."

I reached into my pockets and pulled out a handful of loose bills. I had only about fifteen dollars left. The price tag under the jackalope read "$200."

"Well, I guess I could let it go for a steal," Leslie said. "Fifteen dollars it is."

The image of a happy jackalope and me bounding through a field appeared before my eyes. But it wasn't right.

"Leslie, I can't do that," I said, pocketing the money. "This is too beautiful. And it would be disrespectful to me—and to Aloysius—to let you do that."

There was a cough from the doorway.

We looked back. Jo was leaning against the jamb, wiping grease from her hands onto a rag.

"Rusty back and ready?" Gabe asked.

"Hear for yourself," Jo said, nodding her head behind her. We could hear Sam gunning the engine. She gave out a loud "WHOOOOOPPP!!!"

I patted the jackalope a final time. "Farewell, fair Aloysius," I said. "We must depart on our quest."

Jo tucked the rag into her back pocket.

"How about we work out a deal? Les, you open to that?"

"Always. Bargain is my middle name."

"It is, actually," Jo said.

"Long story." Leslie smiled. "But what bargain are you suggesting, cousin?"

"I've got to be back at school, and you were planning on driving me this weekend. Which means closing up the store, and gas and all that. But Sam has a car."

Gabe and I traded a look.

Leslie began to nod. "So we can exchange the jackalope for a ride to ASU. Hmmm." He rubbed his chin.

"That's not really my decision to make," I said. "It's Sam's car."

"Sam already said yes, so if I drive back with her

instead of making Leslie do it, a stuffed dead rabbit seems like an even exchange for my cuz to make."

"Sounds good to me," Leslie said.

I still didn't think it was quite fair enough.

But then Jo clinched the deal. "And Sam says that you two are amazing at finding the best ice cream places. And that Zed here knows all the words to 'Single Ladies.'"

"Bracket 'Put a Ring on It'!" I shrieked. "And I know the dance moves too!" I began shuffling and waving my hands in front of my face.

Gabe groaned. "Please, no."

Jo smiled. "Sing along in the car with me and that's also worth a lot—Leslie has a strict 'no music while driving' policy, so we're not the best road-trip companions. I know you were being nice," she said to Leslie, "but this'll be much better, and you won't have to leave the store."

He smiled, reached up and carefully plucked Aloysius from his perch. "Seems like a fair deal to me."

He handed him to me. My eyes definitely teared up this time. Part hare, part deer. Something that doesn't exist IRL but should. "It's a miracle," I said.

Leslie laughed.

I looked at Gabe. "Even if the historian beats us to the book, at least I have a real jackalope to bring home with me."

Sam's voice boomed from somewhere behind Jo.

"Let's move it, losers! The Dolly Carton Express is packed and leaving in two minutes!"

"Packed?" I said.

"She's a pro," Gabe replied.

"And she's not kidding about leaving," Jo said. "My stuff's already in the trunk."

Leslie walked over and gave Jo a giant hug. "You get more of those straight As and make us all proud," he said.

"I'll do my best. See you in a few weeks."

"Not if I see you first."

We marched out to the car, but as we passed the computer, I secretly tucked the fifteen dollars into the tin on the desk.

Gabe saw me. "You'd better have a good run of gender-guessing or you are going to owe me big time."

I kissed Aloysius on the head. "Worth the risk," I said.

Dolly Carton, in all her glory, sat in front of the store. Sam was doing some last-second trunk reorganizing.

"Don't even think about chucking my sweaters!" I said.

"What do you think we used as rags when we were fixing the car?" she replied. But she was smiling.

I got in and used the middle seat belt to safely secure Aloysius in place.

Jo hopped into the passenger seat. Unexpectedly, she held up the walkie-talkies Jimi had given me.

"I found these in the trunk. They work?"

I laughed. "My brother 'fixed' them. Which usually means they work as paperweights."

She had opened the back of one and was fiddling with the wires.

"Actually, whoever did this is pretty smart. He added an antenna from a cellphone, which increases the range a lot." She put the cover back on and pressed a button. "And it's way quieter now. Might come in handy."

I was too shocked to speak. Jimi had fixed something and made it work better?

Jo plugged in her music player. "As soon as we're back on the highway, it's time for 'Single Ladies'!"

Gabe put on his headphones.

Sam got into the driver's seat.

"The quest is back on!" I yelled.

"Seat belts!" Sam announced. She started the car. "We're leaving in three, two—"

She looked in the rear-view mirror.

"What in the actual heck is THAT?"

I stroked Aloysius's fur. "Say hello to our new mascot."

CHAPTER 25

Happy

We passed a road sign that said "Happy, Texas, 10 miles," a name that scored very high on the Zed cool-o-meter, TBH.

We'd been on the road for a few hours, with a stop for lunch and ice cream.

The luck of Aloysius had been on my side as I'd successfully predicted that the kid at the counter would call me "girl."

6–6.

But I was more interested in watching Jo and Sam.

They kept leaning close and whispering to each other. At first, I was worried that they were passing intel about the car—the way my parents always whisper to each other when there's stuff they don't want us kids to hear.

But so far, Dolly Rusty Carton Raccoon—or DRCR—had only been making the normal scary noises and whines.

So I think they were whispering sweet nothings.

"Oh. My. Goodness," I said to Aloysius. "That is so cute!"

Aloysius suggested I share this with Gabe.

I reached over and tapped him on the shoulder. He lifted one of his headphones. Another opera leaked out.

"What?" he asked.

"Have they moved closer to each other in the front seat?"

"What?"

"Are you even listening to me?"

"I'm trying to listen to *Carmen*."

"How can you listen to opera when there's a real-life romantic drama happening right before your very eyes?"

"Easy," Gabe said. "Like this." He put the headphones back on.

"You have no sense of romance."

"What are you talking about back there?" Sam called.

"The trip," I lied. Well, it was only sort of a lie.

"I was telling Jo about the coordinates," Sam said. "But I explained that we have no idea where the next stop is supposed to be. I got that right?"

Jo turned around. "Sam says all the other clues were place names?"

"Arcadia. Huzzah. Mantua. But this one isn't."

"Zed-splain it," Sam said.

Well, since they were asking for my expertise, or Zed-spertise, how could I refuse?

"The stanzas in the poem Taylor left behind link to specific chapters," I began. "Considered together, they've pointed to towns and places where clues are hidden. I think they might all have been places where Taylor felt comfortable somehow." I stopped for a moment, imagining the author sitting and reading in front of Lysander's grave, or partying with the crowd in Huzzah all those years ago.

"Focus," Sam called.

I shook my head. "Sorry. But the last stanza and fragment don't seem to do the same thing."

"Why not?" Jo asked.

"Well, the stanza is clearly about Yves Lanois. He's a werewolf, the last of the four great monsters in Taylor's book. The chapter is also about Yves and Lysander, the vampire, and their first date."

(Did Jo and Sam exchange another look when I said that? Yes.)

I recited perhaps my favorite bit from the fragments:

They dined together for the first time. But the dinner was so much more than just a meal.

How sad are the humans who see food as fuel, Yves thought. How much life they miss. How much joy.

The clouds obscured the light of the heavens, allowing the vampire and the werewolf the time to enjoy the meal and the company.

The chef delighted and surprised them with dishes designed for their particular tastes. For Lysander, the sanguine perfection of flying things. For Yves, the bounty of the forest, the prizes of the hunt.

Spurred on by the transcendent food, they moved from pleasant chat to deeper conversation as they discussed good and evil and dined on plant and beast.

A perfect synthesis of the delights of the earth and of the mind—and of the soul.

Soon, like the Ipomoea alba *that surrounded their table, their love bloomed.*

And then . . . they kissed.

Jo instantly endeared herself to me by saying, "That is so beautiful! No wonder you fell in love with this book."

Gabe had now taken his headphones off. "The *Ipomoea* is the key here. It blooms only at night."

"Like a werewolf," Jo said, increasing her Zed rating exponentially.

"Yes!" Gabe replied. "It's actually called the moonflower in English, which is in the last stanza of the poem. And the specific one the werewolf mentions is found in only a few places in the world, including the US southwest."

"But why Texas?" Jo asked. "I thought you were heading for New Mexico?"

"We know we have to end up in New Mexico," I said, "but right now, the coordinates give us this huge chunk of the state. So we need one more number to pinpoint exactly where we need to go."

Gabe jumped in. "And the flower doesn't really bloom west of Texas because it needs moisture, and once you get too far west, it's all desert."

"And Gabe discovered one other cool thing about Texas flowers that Taylor might have been hinting at: the state flower is the bluebonnet."

"In Latin, the *Lupinus texensis*, or Texas wolf flower."

"Texas it is!" Jo said.

"Where we are now," I added.

"Is the moon part significant?" Jo asked.

"We think it's possible that they're eating under a full moon, but Yves doesn't transform because of the cloud cover."

Gabe nodded. "Why else put that detail in there? It has to be night because vampires can't be out during the day."

"And werewolves can't be caught with a clear full moon," Jo said.

"Bingo," I said. "But that's as far as we got. There's no Moonlight, Texas, so we're stumped."

Jo thought for a bit. "Austin has these things called moonlight towers. They're like giant lamps."

"Yeah. We saw those when we were doing research," I said. "But Austin is in the wrong part of the state."

"How?"

"Distance," Sam said. "It's something I noticed as the driver. Each stop has been about the same number of hours apart. And if we draw a line from where we've been to where we're heading, it cuts across north Texas, not south."

"It all makes sense," Jo said. She turned back around, and I saw her check the rear-view mirror.

"Hmm," she said.

I turned to look out the back window, but I couldn't see anything weird.

"What did you see?" Sam asked.

"Probably nothing." But Jo kept staring at the mirror.

Then she stopped, and she and Sam exchanged a glance.

Now they were definitely doing the parental "act cool in front of the kids" thing.

Sam quickly changed the subject.

"All that food talk is making me hungry," she said.

Jo's face lit up. "I know the perfect spot. It's a little off the main road, just past Happy. An old hippie kind of place. A little dated, but it is amazing!"

"Amazing how?"

"You'll see."

CHAPTER 26

Moonlight

Fry bread was not something I had ever experienced before.

Now it was all I wanted to eat for the rest of my long and amazing life.

The diner we stopped at was called Jennie's, and Jennie turned out to be, as she told us, the "cook, waiter and head bottle washer."

She was also the first person to notice the blue, pink and white horizontal stripes on my leggings.

"Awesome trans flag pattern," Jennie said as she showed us to our booth.

I stopped walking and broke into a huge smile.

"I have an apron with the same pattern," she explained.

She also immediately used they/them pronouns when seating us. She took our orders for drinks, winked at me, then turned to Sam. "Do you think *they'd* like fry bread?"

Sam smiled. "I think *they* would love that. Zed?"

Jennie turned back to me. "But seriously, would you like some fry bread?"

I looked at Jo. "You were right. This place is amazing."

When the fry bread came, it was crunchy, soft, chewy—sort of like if you deep-fried a cloud.

We also ordered a tableful of other delectable dishes. Corn tortillas and a green salsa. Squash in a mole sauce. Beans and rice with a tangy zip at the finish.

"A werewolf gourmet would love this place!" I said.

We ate in silence, except for brief exchanges about how wonderful everything was. Jennie, now sporting her trans flag apron, went back and forth between us and the kitchen, reappearing regularly with some tray of veggie delights.

Finally, completely stuffed, I sat back in my chair and took in the restaurant itself.

Jo was right—it looked a little old. Not rundown, but with decor from a different era. There were faded pictures of old cars covering wood-paneled walls. One whole wall was filled with license plates. I quickly spotted plates from Arizona, New York, Ohio, British Columbia. But there were also plates from Alaska, Hawaii and even Ireland and Germany.

Jennie saw me looking around. "My moms founded this place a long time ago," she explained.

"Some of the decorating needs a little updating. But it's a full-time job just running the place."

"Did you say 'moms'?"

She nodded. "Let's just say the traditional road-house wasn't as . . . uh, welcoming as they wanted. They wanted a safe space for people on the road to come and enjoy a good meal without looking over their shoulders the whole time. So they filled that niche with this place. It was all very chic at the time."

"I'm not sure license plates were ever chic," I said with a chuckle. "Cool? Yes."

"The license plates were little thank-yous that people would leave behind. A few were even mailed to us years later. A lot of bars around here do this, but these were different. That's why I've never taken them down."

"Different?"

"It was comforting to look at the wall and know that you were not alone. There was a community of people like you, and it was a global community."

I sat and stared at the wall with a sense of wonder. Every person who had left or sent a plate was some-one who had found community here.

Somebody like Taylor writing that book.

"So was one of your moms named Jennie too?" Gabe asked.

"No. My moms were Bernice and Hazel."

"Sound like hurricanes," I said.

Jennie snorted. "Pretty accurate, actually. Bernice died when I was in chef school. Hazel made me promise I'd make the place my own if I wanted to keep it going. So after she died, I changed the name from the Moonlight Diner to Jennie's Diner."

Gabe spat out some of the cola he was drinking. I sat bolt upright.

"Moonlight?"

"That was the original name. It became a kind of secret that people would pass along about a safe place on the road through these parts. 'The Moonlight has a varied menu' was code for 'You can eat there safely.' And if someone you weren't sure about asked, you'd say, 'The Moonlight is a dump.' That was a total lie, by the way. Hazel was a certified *cordon bleu* chef."

All the pieces were coming together perfectly. This was exactly the sort of place Taylor might have sat to write. This was home to the same community the book embraced. The food was amazing and always had been. Yves Lanois's kind of restaurant. The postcards in Huzzah were from a General Wolf and said "Come dine with me."

This *was* the final place Taylor wanted us to go.

Gabe and I ran over to the license plates.

"Where was Yves from?" Gabe asked.

"Luxembourg," I called.

I ran my fingers up and down the rows of plates. I

must have hit all fifty states and a dozen other countries before Gabe cried out, "FOUND IT!"

I ran over.

There it was—an almost square black metal plate tucked into a spot between an ancient jukebox and the polished wooden bar.

"LUX" was stamped in white letters above the plate's numbers, which were also in chipped white paint.

If we were right, the final parts of the coordinates were now ours.

Gabe pulled out his notebook and wrote in the final sequence:

33.1284N
107.2528W

Jennie walked up beside us. "That was one of the plates we were mailed."

"Do you remember who mailed it?"

She smiled. "I was so young when most of these were put up, but this one . . . it was odd. Even Hazel thought it was odd. The plate had come in a plain envelope with no return address. But there was a note inside and a dried flower. The note said something like 'Thanks for the wonderful meal,' and it was signed with this French-sounding name."

"Yves Lanois?"

"Something like that. I was only a young kid then. I just remember that it sounded French."

"Do you still have the flower?" Gabe asked. "Maybe it was the moonflower!"

Jennie laughed. "No. That was lost a long time ago. The note's lost too. But that's the cool thing about license plates—they can last a long time."

But I knew we didn't need the note or the flower. The numbers on the plate were the key.

I asked one final question very carefully.

"Has anyone else been here looking for this plate?"

"Maybe someone with big feet?" Gabe added.

Jennie thought for a second.

Gabe and I held our breath.

Finally, she said, "Not since I've been here full time. And definitely not recently."

Gabe and I exhaled.

The historian was either behind us or on the wrong track. Maybe he *was* headed to South Carolina!

We hugged the heck out of Jennie, then ran back to the booth to tell Sam and Jo the news.

Chapter 27

Truth?

That night, we splurged and rented rooms at a nearby motel recommended by Jennie.

But I didn't sleep much.

I kept whispering excitedly to Gabe, even though he'd insisted we needed to rest.

How he could even sleep was beyond me.

"I wonder what the book will look like. Do you think Taylor drew pictures? How many more chapters are there?"

"Go to sleep, Zed."

"Sleep? I can't believe Sam and Jo wouldn't let us drive through the night. Sam wouldn't even plug in the coordinates!"

"Good night." Gabe put his headphones on.

"Fine," I said. I reached over and grabbed my herbal tea from my mug warmer.

But I stayed up, whispering to myself, "The door was open, and he was unsure of how to proceed," over and over. It was another line from Lysander's chapter.

I felt the same way Lysander must have felt the night before his dinner date with Yves.

I shivered. Tomorrow I would also finally find out what happened in the Battle of Thistlethorn!

Oh! And what happened after Lysander and Yves's first kiss!

OH! OH! And if Cassandra and Marion ever found each other!

Or—and this must have been Gabe rubbing off on me—whether the plants Lysander and Yves found could heal Marion's undead wounds.

All the possibilities swirled around in my brain, rising and falling like a grand orchestra of ideas.

Finally, the sun rose. I waited until its rays reached the tops of the trees outside the window before I sprang up to wake everyone.

I wrapped myself in my comforter and pounced on Gabe.

He only stirred, so I pulled his pillow out from under him. A trick I got from my younger sister Lillian, who—I had learned firsthand—was extremely good at waking people up. Dad called her the Human Alarm Clock.

Gabe blinked for a second, then bolted upright, arms raised in the air.

"I'm up!" he said.

Now that he was awake, I could see the excitement in his eyes too.

"Race you to get ready!" I yelled.

He jumped out of his sheets and started to take off his pajamas.

I threw away the comforter with a flourish, revealing my already fully dressed magnificence.

"Aw, that's unfair!" he said.

"Sorry, Gabe! You should have known I would be prepared. I picked out this outfit before we even left on this trip!" I was wearing a large crewneck sweater with a classic Dracula face on it. My sweats were Memphis print but in Gothic vampirish red, gold and black.

I grabbed one of Jimi's walkie-talkies from my backpack. I had slipped the other into Sam's bag the night before and turned it on. Now I turned mine on too and pressed the Talk button.

"GOOD MORNING! LET'S GO FIND THE MONSTER'S CASTLE!!!!"

Sam pounded on the wall, and I knew I'd been successful. Jo was right: the walkie-talkies did come in handy.

I slid mine back into my pack.

"Now to breakfast!"

Gabe and I shot out the door.

Soon, we were back at Jennie's, enjoying the most

231

amazing hash browns in the world. She'd opened early just for us.

Sam and Jo were sitting together—closely, I noticed—on the other side of the table.

I swallowed a mouthful of perfectly prepped spuds and gave a satisfied smile. "Jennie, you are a culinary genius," I said.

"Thanks so much! The omelets will be up soon." Then she was off to the kitchen.

"Any chance we can get the rest to go?"

"Sorry, Zed," Sam said. "We're not rushing. We're already up earlier than any human should be."

"But we need to move!"

"I thought your amazing brain needed nourishment."

"That's a good point."

"And I need coffee," Jo said. "I'm like Les—no life in this corpse until at least my second cup."

Jennie seemed to magically appear with a carafe.

"Fair trade from friends of mine in Costa Rica," she said.

I didn't drink coffee, but it smelled amazing.

Then I did a drum roll on the tabletop.

"Sam, where does your GPS say we're heading?"

She plugged the coordinates into her phone, then stared at it like it was broken.

"That can't be right."

"What can't be?" I asked, straining to see the screen.

"Truth or Consequences?"

"Truth or what?" Gabe said.

She passed her phone across the table.

"The coordinates say we're heading to someplace called Truth or Consequences, New Mexico. That sounds made up."

"No, it's real," Jo said. "Although there's not much there. It's named after an old radio show. Apparently, they ran some nationwide contest back in the 1950s, offering to bring the show to any town that would change its name to Truth or Consequences. Used to be called Hot Springs. My grandparents would sometimes go there for vacation. They actually do have hot springs—and this big festival commemorating the radio program every spring."

"That is the weirdest bit of trivia I have heard on this trip," Sam said. "And that's saying a lot with these two along for the ride."

"Three," I said. "Don't forget Aloysius." I'd smuggled him into the restaurant and now raised his head above the tabletop.

"I wish I *could* forget that thing. It gives me the creeps," Sam said.

"Mission accomplished." I stroked the jackalope's fur.

Jennie returned numerous times with more coffee and omelets that melted in the mouth.

Then, finally, we were off.

. . . .

To get to Truth or Consequences, you actually head off the highway and drive through a couple of wild-life refuges.

They were lush and green, but the rest of the landscape was brown and desertlike. The occasional cactus sprung up on the side of a low rolling hill.

We were heading into town when Sam passed me her phone.

"Guide us home," she said. "But don't use up all my data."

At some point, we left the main street and began driving on a rocky road. DRCR bumped and swayed as Sam slowed down to lessen the shock.

I didn't see exactly where we were heading because I was focused on the phone, watching the GPS coordinates like a countdown clock.

The road grew bumpier.

"We're here!" I said at last as the numbers aligned with our code.

"We are?" Sam sounded skeptical, but she stopped the car and turned off the engine.

Gabe rolled down his window.

Silence. Except for the breeze and a few chirping birds.

I looked up from the phone.

I'm not sure what I was expecting, but it wasn't what I saw.

Instead of a bustling town or even a wide-open desert plain, I saw a lone brick building in the middle of a field. Bushes and cacti spread off into the distance. The building was only one story high. I couldn't see a door or any windows. The red brick was faded and had been pockmarked by the wind. The orange roof tiles shimmered in the heat. The building looked old and abandoned.

"This is a Monster's Castle?" Jo asked. "Looks more like a monster's chimney."

She had a point.

"Maybe we need to take a closer look?" I said.

Sam leaned back in her seat. "You and Gabe have fun. I need a nap."

"Good idea," Jo said. She put her head on Sam's shoulder, and in just seconds they were snoring away.

"I guess it's just you and me, Gabe," I said.

We got out of the car and quietly closed the door.

As we approached the building, we noticed signs of life. There was actually a well-maintained flagstone path that led around the building. The brick on that side seemed less worn. The building was also bigger than it looked from the car—it stretched back at least a hundred feet.

"Almost like an optical illusion," Gabe said. "Seems like a tiny old building from one side and a huge one from the other."

"But you have to walk around to see that," I said.

"And there *are* windows here," Gabe said.

"And there's a door!"

The door was tucked into a cavity in the brick. You had to be almost right in front of it to know it was there.

I gasped. "The doorknob, Gabe. It's brass. Like in Lysander's chapter!"

He ran over.

"Maybe this is it!" he said.

"It has to be. Shall we?"

We put our hands on the doorknob together and turned.

There was a slight rush of cool air, and the door opened wide.

CHAPTER 28

The Gate

As surprising as the outside had been, the inside was even more unexpected.

Row upon row of polished wooden bookcases.

Each shelf packed with books.

If *The Monster's Castle* was here, it was going to be hard to find.

We stepped inside.

The door closed with a hush behind us. Then total silence.

"It's a library!" I said in a quiet voice.

"And what a library!" Gabe said. "It's beautiful!"

"What is it doing in the middle of nowhere?"

"*The Monster's Castle* must be here!"

I walked over to the first bookcase and ran my fingers along the spines.

A few were the kind of leather-bound books you might expect to see behind glass in a library.

But most were worn paperbacks.

Some with cracking spines.

But all carefully organized by subject and lined up in perfectly straight rows.

Amazing titles immediately popped out.

GILA the Destroyer!

The Monster Calls at Midnight.

The Haunting of Chicken Ranch.

The Dark Looked Back.

"They're all about monsters," I said. "This is the greatest collection I've ever seen. These books are famous!"

Some of the books, like *The Vampyre's Journey*, I'd actually read. But I'd read them as e-books. I didn't even know physical copies still existed.

"This one, *The Ghoul's Guide to Ghosting*, is so old there's only a few remaining copies in the whole world. And they're all in private collections."

But as much as I searched, no *Monster's Castle.*

"Wow," Gabe said, poring over the titles on another shelf. "These are all about botany."

I walked over. He had pulled a thick hardcover down and placed it on an oak table. There was a wooden stand to put the book on so you could open it without damaging the spine.

Gabe carefully placed the book down and opened it gently. His eyes grew incredibly wide. There were pages of Latin (of course) and faintly colored prints of leaves and flowers.

"This is an original Linnaeus!" he said. "He was the founder of modern botany. This is amazing!"

"And *this* is an original Higgins! And an original Bernard!" I started pulling books off the shelves to show Gabe.

Just then, I heard someone cough behind us.

"Aah!" I yelped, startled. I whirled around quickly, dropping some of the books.

"Oh no, I'm so sorry!"

I bent to pick them up, and they did too.

"It's okay," they said, and we both straightened up.

Standing in front of me was a person with short gray hair in a three-piece tweed suit. They had a watch chain that went from their belt to their pocket, and they were smiling at me. I liked them instantly.

"Welcome to my library." Their voice was soft and melodic.

"YOUR library?" I said, eyes wide.

They nodded, still smiling.

"I don't get a lot of people out here. But I see you are enthusiasts yourselves. Do you know about that one?" they asked, gesturing to one of the books in my hands.

"*The Leviathan Wakes*?! Of course! I've wanted to read this my whole life. This obsessed sea captain battling this giant sea monster. I mean, just look at the cover!" It showed a giant black whale-like creature swallowing a ship. "SO COOL!"

Gabe leaned close to my ear. "Zed, shh! This is a library, remember?"

"Oh, was I yelling? Sorry."

The librarian smiled. "That's perfectly okay. I like your excitement. And this is not that kind of library. . . ?" They cocked their head at me with a questioning look.

"Zed! My name is Zed. And my pronouns are they/them/theirs!"

"And so are mine, Zed! I love that name, by the way. Did you pick it yourself?"

I thought they could not possibly get any more awesome, but they had!

"Yes! And this is Gabe!"

The librarian gave a little bow. "Nice to meet you both. Now tell me, how did you get all the way out here?"

"We drove," I said, "all the way from Happy! And before that, Arcadia, except our car broke down, so we had to stop over in Okay—"

Gabe interrupted. "Yeah, we were following the clues from the poem!"

"Poem?" said the librarian, arching an eyebrow. "What poem?"

Gabe and I took turns filling them in on the whole story. They stood in front of us, hands behind their back, listening and occasionally asking questions. We showed them the postcards from Jerry, and I told them about Aloysius. When we finally got to the end of our story, Gabe and I were out of breath.

But I had one last question.

"So is it here? *The Monster's Castle*? It has to be, right? Do you have it? Can we see it? Can we take pictures? Can we read it?"

The librarian put their hand to their face and tapped their chin in thought.

"Hmmm. *The Monster's Castle*. We don't have any book by that title here, I'm afraid."

"Oh," I said, deflating. "Wait—did someone else get here and take it already?"

"No. It's just not here."

"Oh," I said again.

"Oh," Gabe said.

Just like that, it was over.

I have never, ever felt worse.

Not when I thought the trip wasn't going to happen. Not when I thought the historian was going to get to the book first. Not in the brief moment when I thought he had. Not when I yelled at Gabe. Or when I yelled at Sam.

Not even when the car broke down and I thought I was going to die.

I thought about all the things that had led up to this moment. All the time and the effort. I could see by the look on Gabe's face that he was having the same thoughts.

We had never failed more colossally. I noticed Gabe had started crying. I touched my own face and realized it was wet as well.

"Now, now," said the librarian, putting their hands on our shoulders. "Come over to my desk, and I'll make you some tea. You've come a long way and had such thrilling adventures. Don't leave just yet."

I opened my mouth to protest, but only a squeaky noise came out, so I just said, "Okay."

"Sure," said Gabe beside me.

The librarian led us over to a far corner of the library. There were two old leather armchairs and side tables laid out next to a beautiful large oak desk. The desk had an old-fashioned lamp and a potted flower sitting on it.

The librarian moved the chairs so they were facing their desk and motioned for us to sit. I did, but Gabe went up to the flower.

"This is an incredible orchid," he said. "It's so beautiful."

I saw that Gabe was right. It was delicate, with tiny green flowers just blooming on the end of a long curved stem.

"Thank you. I'm very interested in flowers," they said. "It's known as the Hawaiian bog orchid. Not the prettiest name, but such a beautiful flower."

"The Latin name is prettier," Gabe said. "*Peristylus holochila*."

The librarian beamed. "Exactly."

"It's incredibly rare. You must be an amazing gardener to keep it alive. It's so strange to see it here."

"I guess you could say I like to give strange and beautiful things a home." They laughed slightly and gestured around. "If you couldn't tell. But you must be an amazing gardener as well, Gabe. It's partly why I'm so intrigued by your story. I'm incredibly impressed that you figured out all those clues about plants."

"Thanks," Gabe said, but his shoulders slumped.

"And, Zed, as you can tell, I also like monster stories. And you were able to solve all those clues. Fabulous."

"Thanks," I said weakly. But I didn't feel fabulous. All I could think was that maybe the whole story had been a hoax. Maybe the book wasn't even real in the first place.

The librarian noticed I was still crying, and they clucked their tongue at both of us. "You two need to recognize what you achieved together. Maybe the tea will help."

They disappeared behind a shelf, leaving me and Gabe alone.

"Well, partner, I guess this is it," Gabe said.

He pulled out a tissue pack from one of his pockets and gave me one. We both honked our noses. I shared my awful thought.

"What if the book is a jackalope? Cool and awesome,

245

but just a hoax? What if it was never meant to be found at all?"

He shook his head. "No. The coordinates led us here for a reason. It's too odd a place not to be the home of *The Monster's Castle*."

"Do you think the librarian is lying to us?" I asked.

"No," Gabe said. "But I just don't get it. We followed all the clues! I don't see how we could be wrong. Maybe we need to keep looking at the shelves?"

I was too miserable to reply. The thought of returning home empty-handed made me shiver. My whole family coming up and asking me how it went? I would have to tell them it had all been a waste of time.

The librarian returned with a teapot and two dainty teacups.

"Okay, let this steep for a bit," they said.

"I'm sorry, but I'm not in the mood," I said.

They put the teapot and cups down on the desk. "Milk or sugar?" they asked.

Gabe raised his hand and said, "I take honey, if you have some."

"Well, that does sound good," the librarian said. "I make my own, actually. I have some in the back. Zed? Honey?"

I nudged my teacup but couldn't find the energy to say yes or no.

The librarian smiled at me. "Come now, don't look so down. You achieved so many great things. Together. It's very impressive."

Gabe and I looked at each other and smiled weakly. It was true. We had worked together to solve the puzzle. It wasn't our fault that the puzzle had turned out to be unsolvable.

"And there might be a way I can help."

"But you can't," I said, picking at a loose thread on my sweater. "You said the book's not here."

"Ah, yes. That is true. But while I was in the kitchen, I remembered something else I think you might like. It's a book about plants and monsters. I was looking at it only this morning. Now where did I put it?"

They raised their head and took in the room.

"What kind of plants?" Gabe asked.

"This type of orchid, for example," they said. They used a finger to gently adjust the plant. "Beautiful how it turns in the light, no?"

Gabe nodded.

"What type of monsters?" I asked.

"All kinds. Such as the dragon on my lamp." They

pointed to the iron lamp on the desk. The stem was a twisting fire-breathing dragon.

"That's awesome!"

"Thank you," the librarian said, nodding. "Now, where did I leave that book? I know it's not the one you're looking for, but it might make you feel better."

"Is it here?" I asked.

"Let me get you that honey. Feel free to look around while I'm gone."

They disappeared again. I tried to perk up and wondered what the book could possibly be if it wasn't *The Monster's Castle*.

I looked over at the orchid and the lamp.

I noticed that the dragon's arm was pointing toward the far wall of the library. I followed the line and saw that a reading area had been set up, with two armchairs and a low table with a vase of flowers.

The orchid was also leaning that way. The librarian had turned it to do that!

"Gabe, what flowers are those?" I pointed to the vase.

Gabe squinted. "I need a closer look."

We walked over.

"Zed," he said.

I recognized something in his hushed voice. It was awe.

"What?"

"Look at the flowers." He pointed to the arrangement in the vase. "Rose, moonflower, bluebonnet and ivy," he whispered.

"So? I don't—" I was about to say I didn't get it, but then I did: the plants were all from the book.

"Lysander—blue rose," Gabe said.

"Moonflower and bluebonnet—Yves."

"Ivy covers the monster's castle."

"Covers?" My eyes grew wide and my breath grew short. "What's underneath?"

I got down on my knees.

There was a shelf under the table. Under the ivy.

And on it was a book.

Not a pulpy paperback, but a beautiful leather-bound book. I grabbed it and flipped it over. There was no title or author name on the spine or front cover.

I felt a chill.

"Is this it?"

"Was the librarian just teasing us?"

"Hello!" I called. But there was no answer.

"Open it," Gabe said.

I slowly turned the cover.

It wasn't Taylor's treasure.

In fact, it wasn't a book at all. Or at least, not anymore.

A secret compartment had been cut out of the pages. Green silk was folded over in the hole.

Gabe took a deep breath, pinched the corners of the fabric and pulled it aside.

Revealing not a manuscript but a key—and beneath the key, a hand-drawn map.

We searched the stacks for any sign of the librarian, but they had disappeared.

CHAPTER 29

Consequences

Gabe and I couldn't stop passing the key back and forth.

It was small but ornate. The top was some kind of iron skull. It was awesome. We had no idea what it might open.

The crinkly old map was simpler. Just a set of coordinates and some hand-drawn mounds of rock. The mounds in the middle looked like an actual castle, or maybe a sandcastle, and had a blood-red X drawn overtop.

Here's the thing we'd learned about maps: they get you close to a place, but not standing-on-top-of-an-actual-X close. So we still had to do some searching.

I looked out the car window as we drove farther into the desert. There were a LOT of rocks. And they all seemed to look like the mounds on the map.

"I had hoped this last part would be easier," I said.

Gabe nodded. "Maybe we'll know the perfect mound when we see it?"

I smiled, imagining the scene. "The sun will set just over the top," I said, "sending rays of light flowing. There'll be some awesome dramatic music playing."

"Verdi."

"Disco. And then a fallen angel with wings of fire will raise a hand and point toward a cave, saying—"

Sam broke our reverie. "The sun will be setting in about two hours, angel or no angel. If you haven't found it by then, we'll have to get moving and come back tomorrow. The desert can be pretty darn cold at night."

Jo tapped the dashboard. "And we should stop for gas and oil. Don't want to be trapped out there."

Miles back, we'd passed a sign with a picture of a longhorn skull and the words "Al's Gas—Last Stop Before You Drop." Later, another one read, "Leaving Civilization? Better Visit Al's Station." And finally, "Last Gas Before Your Last Gasp."

I totally wanted to meet this guy!

And Al's rusted sign appeared on the horizon as we made the next turn.

"Shoot," Jo said.

"Is it closed?" Gabe asked.

She held up Sam's cellphone. "No. But we just lost service, so we can't use the phone as a GPS."

Sam didn't seem as concerned. "It's cool. I've got a pretty good idea where we're heading. I'll get us close."

I stared at the heat rippling off the ground, the

miles of cacti and barren rock. I hoped Sam was right.

We pulled into Al's. There was a sign on the pump that read, "Don't pass this gas! Pay inside . . . unless Al's died."

Seriously, this guy!

Sam started filling up.

Jo went to find some motor oil and use the bathroom.

Gabe and I went to see what snacks Al might offer. I also wanted to share my five-star review of his signage.

A little bell dinged as we pushed open the screen door.

"Afternoon," said a deep bass voice from somewhere to our right. "Can I help you all?"

Al, it turned out, was about a thousand years old.

He sat behind a scuffed tile counter with samples of beef jerky, beef rinds and some kind of beef-flavored gum.

"Anything without beef?" Gabe asked.

Al frowned. "Why would anyone want that?" Then he smiled. "Potato chips are back there behind the spark plugs. I think there's a couple of non-beef-flavored varieties."

Gabe went off to look.

"I LOVE your signs!" I said.

He bowed slowly. "Those signs don't lie. I made them years ago, when this really was the only road through the desert. People would think, 'I can skip Al's and make it to the other side.' They'd find them the next morning—lost, sometimes frozen to death. Or bitten by a rattler. Eaten by scorpions. Or coyotes."

Seriously, could Al be any cooler?

He had more. "Or wild dogs. Or stabbed by a cactus."

I heard Sam yell that she was done filling up.

Jo said something I couldn't hear.

"Or trapped under a rockslide. Or—"

Rockslide.

I had an idea. "So, Al, you know this area really well?"

"Yup. Been here all my life. Old as the rocks, some say. Why?"

"Well, we're looking for some kind of castle, and we really want to find it before sunset. But we don't seem to have cell service anymore, so we're kinda guessing about the coordinates."

He listened, nodding. Then he rubbed his chin and looked at me.

"Can't really help you with the numbers. Never had a cellphone myself. But did you say castle?"

"Yes. The Monster's Castle."

He smiled. "I know it very well. Used to hike around there as a kid. But you won't find it on a map, leastways any official map."

Gabe had rejoined us, his arms wrapped around about ten bags of chips. "Why not?"

"Well, the official maps all call it Table Top." He laughed. "Stupid name for something so strange and beautiful. The locals, though, we've always called it the Monster's Castle. Legend has it the cave there is haunted. Makes an awful racket when the wind blows."

As if on cue, the wind began to blow outside, slapping Al's screen door open and shut.

Okay, it was actually Sam and Jo coming in to pay, but it *was* getting windy.

"You've got some amazing tools in your garage," Jo said. "Antiques!"

Al grinned. "Like me. But thank you."

"Is the castle far?" I asked.

"It'd take a little while to walk. But in a car . . ." He got up and motioned for us to follow him. Once at the back door, he pointed. "You see that mountain top there in the distance?"

An almost perfect triangle cut into the sky.

We nodded.

"You head straight for that. You'll have to pull off the main road when it turns. Then you gotta walk, but keep heading for the mountain. Okay so far?"

We nodded again.

"Okay, there'll be a point where you see a river-bed split. One arm cuts to the left and the other heads down to the right. Go left. It'll wind a little, almost like you're in a valley. The Monster's Castle is in among a bunch of other rock formations there."

"Can't miss it, I bet," I said.

Al chuckled. "Oh, you can miss it. If you do, you'll keep walking until your feet wear off. It can be like a maze inside that place, so don't be hasty about it."

He closed the door and shuffled back to his desk.

"That'll be thirty dollars for the gas and oil and another twelve for the chips. The advice is free."

Sam paid him and we headed back to the car, ready for the final leg of our epic adventure. The wind was actually picking up now, sending puffs of dust into the air.

CHAPTER 30

Lookouts

I caught Jo looking in the rear-view mirror as we headed away from Al's and drove even deeper into the desert.

"Okay, what's up?" I asked.

"There's a lot of dust in the air behind us. Just trying to figure out if it's a dust storm . . ."

"Or?"

Jo narrowed her eyes. "Well, if it is a dust storm, we'd better be ready to take cover. But if it's a car—"

"We're being followed," we all said.

Sam almost imperceptibly sped up. "We're almost where Al told us to park."

Jo coughed.

"You okay?" I asked.

She caught my eye in the mirror. "That wasn't me."

The cough came back in spurts.

It was, of course, the stupid car.

"You have got to be kidding me," Sam said. She patted the dashboard. "C'mon, old girl. Just another couple of days."

DRCR gave another hacking noise and then back-fired. A cloud of black smoke filled the view out the back window.

Sam growled and then drove the car onto the shoulder of the road.

The engine stopped coughing . . . because it stopped altogether.

Sam got out and popped the hood. Jo joined her to see what, if anything, they could do to get Dolly running again.

Gabe and I looked at each other.

"Together?" I said, holding up the map.

"Together." He held up the key.

"We'll leave Aloysius here to watch over the mechanics."

Gabe grabbed his backpack from the floor.

We threw in some water and the potato chips and opened the doors.

Sam looked up from under the hood, grease smudged all over her arms. "What do you two think you're doing?"

"You said we're close." I pointed at the horizon. "I can see the riverbed Al talked about right there. We've got some daylight left, and we are *not* waiting to see if the historian is following us."

I stole a look back down the road. Whatever dust had been churned up had settled or blown away. Still, I had an uneasy feeling.

"*Pleeeeeeease*, Sam?"

She turned her head and stared at the horizon.

Jo was grabbing her tools from the trunk.

"Fine, but stay in touch," Sam said. She handed Gabe her cellphone.

"I thought there wasn't any service out here?" he said.

I tried to step on his foot to stop him from saying anything more, but he wasn't standing close enough.

Sam said something I won't repeat. "Maybe there's some over there," she said, kicking the front tire.

But I could see our little side trip evaporating like water on sand.

Then Jo came back like a guardian angel and handed me a walkie-talkie.

She turned the other one on and placed it on the ground next to the car. Mine gave a short squawk, then emitted a low sizzling sound.

"Jimi's boosters actually work pretty well. Keep yours on. If you hear the static stop, you'll know you've walked out of range. Stop and turn back RIGHT AWAY. But you can keep exploring as long as you can hear the static. Deal?"

I looked at Sam. She nodded. "But if we call you to come back, you turn back *immediately*."

"Deal!" I said. I clipped the walkie-talkie to my backpack.

Sam turned to Jo. "And this way, if we *are* being followed, we can keep an eye out—and maybe a couple of arms." She flexed her biceps.

"Lookouts. I like it," Jo said.

My muscles actually relaxed.

"Thanks, you two," I said.

Jo wiped some sweat off her forehead with a cloth. "We'll also get our faithful steed ready for your return with the Holy Grail."

Sam gave me and Gabe love taps on our shoulders. "Go find this treasure."

Gabe hugged his sister. "Thanks, Sis."

We opened a bag of chips, took a handful each and marched off.

CHAPTER 31

The Monster's Castle

The desert plays tricks on you.

Everyone knows about mirages. Like you think you see water ahead, but then it's just heat waves reflecting off a hot surface.

But there are other tricks up the desert's sleeves, let me tell you.

For example, when Gabe and I reached the riverbed, it split just like Al had said it would. But when we looked to the left, the ground seemed totally flat. Cracked like a giant sandy eggshell, but flat.

The right fork, on the other hand, seemed to lead to a bunch of rocky piles like the ones on the map.

We stood at the crossroads, confused.

"Al said left, right?" Gabe said.

"Right."

"You mean go right? Or right, go left, right?"

"Gabe, you're making my head hurt." I turned his shoulders toward the left and pushed. "Let's just trust that Ancient Al knows what he's talking about."

And this is how we discovered the trick.

The land looked flat, but as we walked along, we started sloping downward. What looked like cracked flat earth from above was actually a disguised mini valley of rocky towers and pillars.

"Wow!" we said as we entered this forest of stone.

All the time, the walkie-talkie crackled and fizzed. I turned the volume almost down to zero as the static buzzed off the sides of the rock.

"Sounds too much like a swarm of killer bees calling for reinforcements," I said.

"Or a rattlesnake getting ready to nibble."

"Yeah. I want to be able to hear THOSE things clearly."

You could still hear the static if you strained, which I felt was in the spirit of Jo's command.

The air seemed to get thicker and cooler, and the light fainter, as we walked through the columns of stone. Then we turned a corner, and despite what Al had said, we didn't miss it. And we knew it was the right place.

In a large wide clearing, a pile of rocks unlike any other.

"THE MONSTER'S CASTLE!" Gabe and I said together.

We rushed toward it, lucky not to step on any snakes or killer scorpions.

A breeze rustled the brush, and we heard a low moan from the castle. We stopped and listened.

The breeze picked up and the moan got louder.

The wind paused and the moan stopped.

We walked quickly along the base, looking for the source of the sound. A breeze came up again and the moan returned, low and deep.

"It's coming from behind that boulder!" Gabe said.

We looked behind and found a crack. A Zed-and-Gabe-walking-side-by-side-sized crack!

We knew what we had to do.

We held hands and bowed.

"May the ancient ones who guard the Monster's Castle speed OUR safe passage through its halls."

Then we walked in, tingling all over. It was cool and damp inside, and dark.

"Flashlight?" I asked.

"There's one on Sam's phone," Gabe said. He pulled it out. "Still no service, but it does have a light." He flicked it on. The light revealed a cave about thirty feet long and ten feet wide. The ceiling soared a good thirty feet above us.

There was a hole in the ceiling that rose all the way to the top. I could make out a tiny circle of blue sky.

"There *is* a monster's chimney!" I said.

The breeze resumed, and the low moaning sound echoed down the chimney and off the walls of the cave.

"Like blowing over top of a bottle," Gabe said.

"Cool. Now where's the treasure?"

We ran the light across the walls.

And saw, almost hidden in a pile of rubble against the far wall, a painted stone. We hurried over, and with a delicate finger, I brushed off the years of dust, revealing an unmistakable blood-red *X*.

"Looks like a good place for scorpions," Gabe said.

I trusted his scientific understanding of nature, so I grabbed my pen and super carefully began lifting the stones and pebbles.

Finally, after holding my breath, I heard a scratch as the pen slid across not stone but metal.

My heart raced, and I could feel tears in my eyes as I quickly brushed aside the remaining stones, revealing a plain metal box. It was painted gray and had a small slightly rusted keyhole at the front of the lid. No decoration. No symbols. No etched poem. Nothing to signify this contained anything special, even though inside there might be the only complete copy of the greatest book in the world.

"We did it," I said, standing up and holding the box as gently as I could.

"And we did it together," Gabe said, putting a hand on my shoulder.

"Actually," said a voice from the shadows, "I'll take that box."

CHAPTER 32

History

Gabe and I slowly turned around. I was now clutching the box so tightly my fingers ached. This couldn't be happening.

Not now. Not so close to the end of our quest.

"Put the box down. Slowly." A man's voice. The historian? Here.

A shadow blocked the light from the outside. The setting sun gave the man an eerie orange aura. He was holding something. A long stick, or maybe even a rifle. My knees shook.

"What have you done with my sister?!" Gabe yelled.

"And Jo?"

"They're fine," said the man, raising the stick. "I saw the big black puff of smoke while I was following you. I know a dying car when I smell one. So I stopped down the road and went around them. They're still back there, trying to get that lemon to work again."

He stepped forward, letting in more light.

I could see him now. Tall. Large feet crunched against the stones. The stick wasn't a rifle, thank goodness, but it wasn't much better. He held a heavy blue crowbar in his right hand and tapped it against his open left palm.

"I said, put down the box. NOW."

I hesitated, and he took another step closer.

"Maybe we should do as he says." I turned my head slightly to face Gabe and winked my left eye quickly.

He nodded. I felt him lower his hands. One of them brushed against my backpack.

"I think you're right, Zed." Gabe lifted his right hand. "But first, sir, we'd like some answers."

"I know you didn't come in here with any weapons," the man said. "So you're not exactly in a position to make demands."

I bent down and placed the box at my feet. I spoke with a clear, loud voice.

"Gabe, you and I wanted to find the treasure. We have. But it doesn't matter as long as the world finally knows the truth about what's in this box."

The man took another step toward me. "True. It will see the light of day. And I alone will bask in the glory of that light."

I stood up. "It's yours. No one needs to get hurt."

He actually stopped tapping the crowbar. "I agree. Once I get that box, I'll leave. No one will trust the word of two freaks who have no idea how the real world works, over a trusted academic like me. Especially not two freak *kids*."

Something he said tweaked a memory.

"So wait, why do you want this box so badly?"

He smirked. "To secure my future as a best-selling author. Once I get the final manuscript—the world's *only* copy—I can submit it to my editor as the remaining chapters of my own masterpiece."

I gasped. "You . . . you're Roger Stan! The hack who wrote all those horrible monster stories!"

"The jerk we kicked off the fan site!" Gabe said.

Stan smirked. "For being smarter than the rest of you pathetic sycophants."

I whispered to Gabe, "Is that Latin?"

"It means you're a bunch of slobbering fools!" Stan shouted.

Good, I needed him shouting. The louder the better.

"Taylor is probably long dead. Anyone who's read this book is too. The publishers went bankrupt. No one cares about it except you two! Where are all the other fans, huh? Did they come on this trip? No. Just a couple of dumb kids who don't know any better. No one is going to take your word for anything."

"You really think you can get away with passing this masterpiece off as your own?! No one will believe it!" I shouted.

Roger was close enough now to reach for the box with the crowbar.

"You think I'm a monster, don't you?" he said, leaning forward and using the bar to grab the box.

"I would never insult a monster with that comparison." It was proof Roger had no love for this book, no understanding of what it could mean to people who needed a story like this.

I understood in a flash that the librarian had led *us* to the map for a reason. They trusted us. Trusted us to do right by Taylor's memory. To do justice for the misunderstood monsters in the book.

I hoped even harder that my plan was working.

It was time to find out.

"You reached the library before us, didn't you?" I said. "But the librarian sent you away with nothing."

Stan stopped dragging the box. He stood up, his face twisted in a sickly grin.

"No, I got there after you. I lost track of the route after you stopped posting stuff on the site. And when you didn't take the bait and head to South Carolina, I figured you did know where you were going. So I followed."

"You're @Hi_Its_Another!"

"It's an anagram. I'm clever that way."

"The historian," Gabe said.

"But you're right. The librarian wouldn't give me anything. Said only someone who loved both monsters and plants could crack the code. Said I didn't love either. But I knew you two did, and they must have told you where to go next. So I followed you again. And I also packed my trunk with some rare volumes from the collection. I do love money."

"Did you hurt the—"

"No need. That old freak just sat and watched me. Although with the money I make off this book deal, I might just buy the place and then burn it to the ground. After I loot even more of those collectibles."

He bent over and picked up the box.

Now I smiled.

"Gabe, any chance you've got all this?" I said.

"Yup." He held up Sam's phone. "Recorded the whole rant. Good thing too, because Roger here told us everything."

Stan scowled. "There's no service out here, you fool. That evidence is useless. Now give me the phone." He lifted the crowbar.

That's when Gabe held up the walkie-talkie in his other hand. "True. I can't upload your nice speech yet. But there's more than one copy," he said.

Stan stopped, the crowbar hovering at his side.

"What do you mean?"

"We worked out a backup plan on the walk here," I said.

Gabe waved the walkie-talkie. "When Zed winked at me, I hit Record on the cellphone, but I also pressed down the Talk button on this. And I tapped out an SOS in Morse code."

"So?" Stan was clearly having trouble following what was happening. He began to inch forward, crowbar raised.

"So my sister knows what that means. We both know Morse code."

I smiled. "And Jo also knew that she should record whatever came through the walkie-talkie."

"You're lying." He'd almost reached us.

"Nope," Gabe and I said together.

"It doesn't matter anyway," he spat. "By the time they get here, I'll be gone with the manuscript and the money. And you'll be—"

There was a cough behind him as Jo and Sam walked into the cave.

"Nice work, Zed," Jo called, holding up her cellphone. "Got the whole thing here."

Stan whirled around. His head swiveled back and forth between Gabe and Jo. He eyed both phones greedily and smiled.

"That was a stupid plan. Now I can get my hands on both copies. Hand me the phones. Both of them."

"Hold on there, pal," Sam said. "Unless you'd like to have a little conversation with my friends Thelma"—she pointed to her left bicep, then her right—"and Louise."

"And my friend Crowbar doesn't scare you?" he said.

"Call that a crowbar?" Jo said. She reached behind her and pulled out a gigantic wrench. "Does a number on lug nuts. Just imagine what it could do to a talkative academic pinhead."

Now Stan wobbled. The crowbar shook in his grasp. I couldn't tell if it was from fury, fear or both.

"I can't believe I was outsmarted by a couple of kids and two—"

Sam held up a fist. "I don't think you want to finish that sentence. Do you?"

Stan shut up. He was shaking like a leaf now. It *was* fear. He dropped the crowbar, which clanged off the floor.

"Tsk, tsk," said Jo. "What a horrible way to treat a perfectly good tool." She walked over to pick it up.

"The box, please," I said. I held out my hands.

Stan practically threw it at me, then he shoved Jo and ran out of the cave. The last we saw of him, he was scrambling away back up the riverbed.

We watched him go.

"What if he wrecks our car?" Gabe asked.

"Isn't it already a wreck?" I said with a laugh.

Sam and Jo gave each other a high five. "We fixed it, then moved it down the road. That's how we got here so fast."

I looked at Jo, still holding her phone in her hand. "You didn't actually record anything, did you?"

She smiled. "I did once I was standing outside the cave and heard you say to. But that was a good one. And I assume Gabe did actually record?"

Gabe pressed Play on Sam's phone, and we heard the sniveling voice of Stan saying, ". . . smarter than the rest of you pathetic sycophants." He stopped it and smiled.

Sam walked over and gave us each a huge hug. "Smart thinking on the Morse code, little brother— and Zed. Of course, we'd also been calling you for fifteen minutes with no answer, so we were already on our way. Not that you needed us."

"Oops," I said.

Gabe turned the volume on our walkie-talkie back up. The static came back.

"I think you owe Jimi a pretty big thanks," Jo said.

"Agreed," I said. "Now, what say we return to the main plot of our epic story?"

"You do love being dramatic," Sam said.

"You know it!"

"One other thing," Sam asked. "What did that jerk mean about money?"

I smiled and hugged the box, and we walked outside. Gabe leaned over to Sam and Jo, and whispered,
"Taylor supposedly buried money with the manuscript!"

"You're just telling me this NOW?!" Sam yelled,
but Gabe shushed her.

The sun was setting, casting a golden glow over
the scene.

I gently placed the box on top of a flattened boulder.

Gabe stuck the key into the lock.

"Together on three?" I said. "One . . ."

"Two . . ."

"Three," we said together.

Gabe and I turned the key.

There was a loud click, and the lid opened just a
crack.

We held our breath and lifted the lid.

But the box was completely empty.

CHAPTER 33

One Person Alone

Just kidding! *Of course* there was something inside.

Everything we'd been searching for, in fact!

On top was a faded yellow sheet with "The Monster's Castle" written in flowing cursive letters. Underneath, the manuscript. Five hundred neatly typed pages with handwritten notes in the margins.

I lifted it out and kissed it. Gabe did too.

Then we turned to page one and read the words . . .

Lysander St. Clair looked down from the highest window of his home, the Monster's Castle.

I couldn't read any more because my eyes had filled with happy tears.

"Don't let the ink run, doofus!" Sam said.

"And we'd better get moving," Jo said. "Sun is going down fast."

I wiped my eyes on Dracula's face and placed the cover page back on top. I was just about to put the

manuscript back in the box when Gabe noticed the envelope that had been tucked into the pages.

Taylor had written a note on the outside.

Thank you. I knew it would take someone with an incredible open heart to find my beautiful monsters. It is a rare person who can hold a love for both the natural and the supernatural. Perhaps one person alone cannot. All I can hope is that whoever you are, you will share my story with the world.

—H.K. Taylor

Inside the envelope were one hundred crisp hundred-dollar bills.

That got a cheer from Jo and Sam.

Gabe and I looked at each other. "Perhaps one person alone cannot," we repeated. Then we hugged. We carefully closed and locked the box, with the treasure inside, and walked back to the road.

The sun set behind us, golden and pure.

A slight breeze rustled the bushes, and a low moan from the castle whispered farewell.

As we reached the car, one more odd thing happened.

Sam's phone buzzed.

She took it out of her pocket and looked at the screen.

"What the heck?" she said. "Zed, Gabe, you're not going to believe this."

"What?"

"Do either of you know someone with the handle @Times_Lisa?"

One Year Later

@Times_Lisa turned out to be a newspaper reporter named Lisa Velasco. She was the one who'd written the article that mentioned *The Monster's Castle*, so it was incredibly cool that she wanted to talk to us.

She'd been trying to reach me on the fan site, she said, because she'd heard about our quest while researching a follow-up article on tight-knit online fandoms.

And she'd been doing stories on our progress for her newspaper.

In fact, when I logged on to the Taylor fan site from Sam's phone, the new members' meter had turned over a thousand times.

The site was flooded with people who wanted to know more about the story, and about how we'd cracked the code. They were also, it turned out, desperate to read Taylor's masterpiece.

And why wouldn't they be?

The complete version of *The Monster's Castle* was even more incredibly awesome than I *ever* could have imagined.

Gabe and I stayed up all night reading it to each other.

There were a bunch of new characters we had never even HEARD of! Like Sylvia Sargasso. She's a kind of water monster, and one of the coolest beings ever. She has this superpower where she can talk to anyone who comes into the ocean. She's kind of like a Siren, except she doesn't care about luring men to their deaths or anything—although she does love to cause trouble. And she does good too. She warns sea creatures about pollution. She's fiercely protective of her underground lair, and she scares away people who come to fish and dive there.

How does she scare them and protect her home? It's all in the book.

She's no Lysander, but she's still super cool.

Gabe and I agreed that she was one of the best parts of our discovery, since she's a monster and—like him—is totally into underwater plant and animal life. The big nerds.

And it turned out, finding the manuscript was just the start of a different journey.

A year later, Gabe and I were sitting together on a plane. Gabe was on the aisle, holding Aloysius, and I was in the middle, holding the box.

"That's a very interesting container," said the lady at the window.

"Thanks," I said. "It's a gift."

"We decorated it ourselves," Gabe said.

I smiled. It was the same box we'd found holding the manuscript. But we'd decorated it with handmade stickers.

"This one is Lysander," I told the lady, pointing to a vampire sticker I'd made.

"Oh, he looks handsome."

"This one is a bluebonnet," Gabe said, pointing to the blue flower.

"I love those," said the woman. "Very pretty. Who's the present for?"

"That's a long story," I said.

Just then, a voice over the intercom told us to get ready for landing.

And half an hour later, still holding the box, we walked off the plane in Albuquerque and through some sliding glass doors to the arrivals area.

"Sam!" Gabe yelled. He ran over and hugged his sister.

"Jo!" I yelled. She was standing there holding a sign that said "Nerds."

We all hugged.

"Ready?" Sam said.

Gabe and I nodded. "Totally ready."

We walked outside and gasped.

"You got a new car?" I said. "I thought you'd never get rid of that piece of junk."

Sam scowled. "This *is* that piece of junk. The one that helped you find that book!"

"Oh. Hello, Dolly," I said.

"But it doesn't look like Dolly," Gabe said.

Jo patted the hood. "We've made some alterations. Thanks to Taylor's money."

"Now she's no longer known as Dolly Carton." Sam bumped Jo's hip.

"Say hello to Car-ssandra!" Jo said.

I gasped. "You read the book!"

"Uh-huh," Jo said. "We read it together. And you're right—Cassandra is awesome."

"Get inside," Sam ordered. "And put a bag over that creepy rabbit."

"Never," I said.

The drive was about an hour—just enough time to catch up.

"How's Leslie?" I asked.

"Great!" Jo said. "There are these weird monster-loving tourists who keep popping in. They're apparently retracing some lost-book journey a couple of goofy kids did. He's sold a lot of jackalopes."

"Interesting," I said.

Lisa had written a whole long article about our quest, complete with maps and locations and stuff.

"Jennie says the diner is packed every night now," Sam added.

"And Darlene has been able to raise some money to clean Big Blue."

That wasn't all. Jerry had written us postcards. Apparently, there was talk of restarting the summer festival.

And the video of me dancing to "Mashed Potato Time"? Well, that went viral and the song was back on the charts.

I guess the world *was* ready.

"Okay," Sam said, "we're here."

The parking lot outside the library was jammed with cars.

Cars with vampire bumper stickers. Cars with license plates like "MNSTR66."

Gabe and I walked to the door.

Together we put our hands on the brass handle and turned.

People were everywhere, reading books, chatting and drinking tea with honey.

We walked past them, all the way to a big oak desk at the back.

The librarian was sitting there. They looked up and broke into a gigantic smile.

"Zed and Gabe, what can I do for you?"

"We have something we'd like to do for *you*," I said. I slid the box on top of the desk.

The librarian's eyes misted a bit as they took in all the decorations.

Gabe handed the librarian the key. "Take a look inside," he said.

They carefully unlocked the box and opened the lid. Their lips trembled as they reached inside and pulled out a book.

"It's the very first one printed," I said, choking up too. "The publisher sent it to us, and we feel like this is where it belongs. It's just the kind of strange and beautiful thing that could use a home like yours."

The librarian was very quiet as they ran their fingers over the glossy cover.

"The original manuscript is in there too," Gabe said.

"It wasn't here the first time we visited. But it also seems to belong."

The librarian got up and walked over to a shelf. They carefully placed *The Monster's Castle* among the other books.

"I wonder who'll read it first," they said, running their finger down the spine.

"You don't need to?" I asked.

"Is that because you wrote it?" Gabe asked.

They didn't respond.

It was the only unanswered question left from our quest.

Gabe and I looked at each other.

I took a deep breath.

"Are you Taylor?"

The librarian sighed softly and turned back to us with a smile.

"Now how about some tea?"

HOWDY PARDNER

GETTING GABE TO ROCK

BOOORING
FLYING DUTCHMAN!!

Acknowledgments

First of all, we'd like to thank Suzanne Sutherland for bringing this book to fruition. Basil had Zed in their head for a while, but it was the push from Suzanne that got us working together and helped form Zed into the dashing, fabulous kid they are on these pages. (There might even be a little Suzanne in the kick-butt character of Sam.)

We'd also like to thank the great, and tragically gone-too-soon, Sheila Barry. Sheila made all of us better at what we do. She is missed every day.

Dozens of people help make a book a book. Natalie Meditsky and the design crew at HarperCollins deserve a giant thanks.

We'd like to thank the members of our family — spread all over the globe. The support we get for our personal and professional lives is everything.

And one final thanks. A lot of the editing and illustrating of this book happened in a pandemic, and I got through some of the darkest days with the help

of the amazing Drawn to FANtasy gang—led by the DiTerlizzi family—Tony, Ang, Soph, Mimi and Pippin.
Love each other.
Make the world a better place each day.
And listen to each other. You'll learn a lot.

—Kevin

Huge thanks to: my incredible friends and chosen family, Leo, Celia, Sasha, Geena, Kaeli and Manny, Davrielle, Blue and Élie, for everything; I'm so glad we are in this life together. Everyone at Mabel's Fables and at House of Anansi and Groundwood Books for believing in the power of good books and community. Special shout-out to Cindy Ma for not minding being pestered constantly and for being the best hype man this weirdo could ask for! Our fabulous editor, Suzanne Sutherland, who introduced me to the Glad Day Bookshop in Toronto when I was a teen, where I experienced firsthand how life-changing LGBTQ+ literature was and could be. Kit H. for always being up for talking about writing and ideas and wacky characters and everything! There's a lot of you in this book. Erin, Mom, David and my extended family a thousand times over, but especially Kit for knowing exactly what I'm going to say, sometimes even before I say it. The Berot-Burnses for always being a heck of a good time. Grandma and Grandpa Carlin for chats on theatre, baseball and complicated ethical questions. Gram and Grampa S. for understanding the importance of good food and good company—Chez Watson is very much inspired by the warm chaos of a Sylvester gathering. And finally, my dad, my co-author and my creative partner-in-crime, Kevin Sylvester. We really did this thing! Time for a celebratory dance party!

—Basil